The Captive Bride

DAVID PRASHKER

ISBN:061590923X
ISBN-13:9780615909233

A significant number of the tales in this collection first appeared in the quarterly magazine "West Quest", sadly now defunct.

In Lawrence Durrell's novel "The Alexandria Quartet", the character Pursewarden offers a series of short epigrams and aphorisms with the apothecarial advice:

"One to be taken from time to time, as required, and allowed to dissolve slowly in the mind."

That prescription is sound for this volume also.

.

CONTENTS

PREFACE

This book is entitled "The Captive Bride". At different times I've thought of calling it "Myths & Parables", "Riddles & Enigmas", "Puzzles & Paradoxes", "Homages to Rabbi Nachman", "Mazes & Mysteries", "The Wisdom of the Datsmay", and even, though very briefly, "The Book of Conundrums". A title is no more than a signpost, a direction-marker; in the end "The Captive Bride" will do.

I have been writing these "minimal" tales for nearly forty years, and they appear more or less in the order in which they were written; only the last four have been deliberately placed, to make a proper ending, or at least a satisfactory conclusion; and of course the "addenda" are addenda. Reading the later ones again, it seems appropriate that the themes of the first have begun to recur, for eternal recurrence is itself a leitmotif that echoes through the book, and after all there's a strict limit to the number of dreams a man may dream.

"Minimal" should not be misunderstood as "minimalist", which is a literary genre; these are minimal tales in that they have been compressed for optimum density into minimum space, the way cargo is in a ship's hold; in one case hermetically sealed, in another restrained not just to a single paragraph but a single sentence.

Originally I intended only to write a single story, one that would accommodate the universe and thereby suffice for a life's oeuvre (I shan't say which tale it was). Having done so, and found it satisfying despite my failure to achieve what was anyway a vain and foolish goal, I decided to write more. At a certain stage I swore to stop at fifty, but by the time I reached that arbitrary figure I had quite forgotten my resolve, and so went on. Then I swore to stop at ninety-nine, for reasons as much mystical as superstitious, but mostly from the recognition that so many tales can numb a reader after one too many. That resolve too achieved its nemesis (I say "achieved", because a true nemesis is a form of the Immaculate Failure). Then I set my sights on a hundred and one, because 101, when not a torture-chamber, is a numerical palindrome, which for a book like this is a better pretext for discontinuing than any mere round number. The final tally of the tales in this book is actually incalculable – several times there are stories which share the same title, or are sub-tales, or merely alternative permutations of the same basic anagram. So perhaps there is only One Tale, after all, as there is only One God, despite the illusion of multiplicity.

It is the custom among authors to dole out acknowledgements in their frontispieces, in the manner of Oscar winners and academic scholars, both of whom they desire to emulate. For myself I wish to pay tribute to two great masters of the minimal tale and the literary riddle; and to do so in a manner appropriate to this book; not mentioning them by name, but indirectly, by allusion: expressing my esteem for Max Brod, who rescued from the fire what might otherwise have become a proof of Heinrich Heine, and for Adolfo Bioy Casares, whose companionship at lunch was more significant than all the mirrors and all the tigers and all the libraries of eternity.

David Prashker

between the 18th and 19th Iyyar 5773

DREAM-MURDER

That night, Simcha Hurlitz dreamed that he had killed a man. He saw the man's face in intense detail, as if through a magnifying glass or the zoom lens of a camera: the eyes dilated by fear, the lips turned redder than their own redness by the blood that was mingling with his saliva. He saw the man's body, prone and prostrate on what could have been a mound of earth and flowers. He saw the trickle of blood issuing from beneath the man's clothing, though whether caused by knife or bullet or some other weapon was unclear. He saw his own shadow, looming in the moonlight above the corpse, and though he didn't see the deed performed, he knew that it was he himself who was the murderer.

When he awoke, hours before dawn and in a feverish sweat, Simcha could remember every detail of the dream with gruesome vividness; but who the victim was - this he did not know. Yet he supposed the dream to have been authentic, the murder to have been genuine, the victim to have been, not a phantasm, but a previously real, a once flesh-and-blood, an erstwhile living man. For dreams are not films nor fictions, but the truths of the unconscious mind in its torpid state erupting into fleeting and fragmented yet still veracious images. So Simcha knew that he was guilty of the crime of murder; though he had killed only in dream, still the unconscious is as much a part of a man as are his eye or mouth or heart, and what a man is capable of in sleep, surely he is no less capable of perpetrating when he's wide awake? How hard it is to accept such truths about oneself! Simcha felt in his heart a weight of guilt for his dream-crime that was almost too intense to bear. Yet what could he do?

That afternoon Simcha Hurlitz was found dead in the kitchen of his home, the veins of his wrists slashed with a razor-blade. A suicide note beside the body spoke of guilt, and of retribution, and of justice.

ORAL TRADITION

In our village, a great deal of time is wasted every year, arguing as to what is, and what is not, the correct formula for carrying out the rites and ceremonies. The truth is, nobody knows, for what is written down is either ambiguous or contested in its authenticity. Whether at the spring or the mid-winter rites, whether at births or deaths or marriages, the same arguments prevail, the same inconclusiveness is always the conclusion: that we do not, perhaps cannot know what is correct, but in the absence of certainty we nonetheless have Tradition to inform us. It is specious, but sufficient - we do what was done on the previous occasion, so no criticism can be offered.

Thus, in carrying out my part of the ritual, I know that I'm probably doing it wrong, but I also know that it matters not one jot - and not simply because doing it wrong is still better than not doing it at all. Doing it wrong is now, by curious irony, itself a form of correct behaviour. I do it wrong, and in so doing I edify and confirm Tradition. I do it wrong *precisely because my father did it wrong before me*, because he didn't learn it correctly from his father, who had forgotten a great deal of what his father misinformed him, his grandfather not having explained it properly to his son. That grandfather, of course, got it from his father, and everybody knows (this, too, is part of the Tradition; this, too, may well be wrong) that he had entirely misunderstood the radical changes which his father promulgated, assuming them to have been adopted when in fact it's the tradition never to alter tradition, but which ideas he sought to inculcate in his son anyway, partly because the teaching of wisdom is itself a tradition (and the teaching of wisdom must, of necessity and by definition, include the questioning of received wisdom), partly in protest against the tradition he had mislearned from his father, who had passed on erroneously what he did in fact learn from the original, the only written text, which as I say has now been rejected outright for its ambiguity and whose authenticity has anyway been questioned.

THE BOMB

"The child is father to the man"

I am a bomb, one hundred megatonnes of pure apocalypse enclosed in a shiny metal shell, the egg of a supernova waiting to be hatched into life. The sleek, nimble hands of the men who gave birth to me fold together in humility at the glory of their progeny, the ineluctable deus in machina they have created, more powerful even than themselves. Men fear me, like a god, like God Himself - the omnipresent force, the all-powerful Ubermensch, ruler of their universe, brighter than any firework. What do I care who uses me, who gives me the opportunity to live my brief life, who takes me from this steel rack where I am held a prisoner? What do I care about your paltry subterfuges, your human scruples? I cannot pretend to be other than I am. I cannot submit to any authority but that of my own nature. I was born to light up the Heavens, to spread myself like a robe across the Earth. Like all of God's creatures my life has but one imperative, and no one has the right to deny me its execution. I must become myself. I must achieve my full potential. I must fulfil my destiny.

THE MESSAGE

This morning I visited an old man at the hospital in order to give him a message. I sat down on the chair beside his bed and took his hand in mine, for it was a difficult message to communicate, especially to one so old and so infirm. The length of my silence didn't seem to worry the old man however, who took advantage of it to tell me his story. From the words he used I guessed he'd told it many times before.

"When I was a young man," he began, "working as a farmer in the hills of Korazim, the prophet Isaiah visited me one day, to inform me that, on a certain occasion in the future, the Almighty would summon me to perform a great and difficult task. He didn't say what that task would be, nor was he able to name the date. He simply brought me the information, and then he departed.

"Ever since that day I've tried to prepare myself, to be ready. Because I didn't know the nature of the task, I couldn't know for what to prepare myself, and so I've endeavoured to be ready for any and everything. I've learned several languages and studied the teachings of all the prophets. Scarcely a book that's been written have I not read; scarcely a fruit that grows have I not tasted; scarcely a land in all the five continents have I not visited. I've known women and I've known abstinence, just as I've known both joy and suffering, both poverty and wealth, and I can say that my life has not been lived in vain. Even now, at this very old age, my body has lost none of its vigour, my mind none of its agility. It has taken the whole of my life to prepare for this task, but now I fear the Almighty has forgotten me. A part of me no longer believes that it really was Isaiah who visited me - or perhaps it was indeed Isaiah, and he was simply having a joke at my expense. But it doesn't matter. Now I lie here, waiting for death, knowing that I'm worthy of the task, knowing that I shall not now be called upon to perform it."

For a moment his eyes drew closed, and he turned his face aside. Then, once more, he looked up at me, and squeezed my hand. Though his face was full of sadness, on his lips there was the faintest outline of a smile.

"But tell me," he whispered, "what brings you to an old man's bedside?"

"I've come to bring you a message," I replied. "I am the prophet Isaiah, sent to you by the Almighty. The time has now come for you to perform that task. I know that you are ready."

The old man looked deep into my eyes, incredulous. I could see that he thought that I was merely humouring him. In his eyes there was a look of grave despair. I let go his hand and covered his face with the sheet.

THE LOTTERY

Science and technology had progressed to such a point that all things men could want were now provided. School children learned in history lessons about famine, drought and poverty, but by now these concepts had become so distant, so abstract and anachronistic, as to be virtually incomprehensible. Such were the gluts and surfeits of all forms of produce - food and clothing, computer games and holiday villas, TV shows and collections of hagiography - such was the cheapth of travel, that Mankind had virtually overcome the state of wanting altogether, and it was true to say that, sadly, a universal apathy that was approaching atrophy had started to set in.

And yet, even if there were no longer wants, there remained needs. To clean the streets, to gather in the harvests, to construct the shopping precincts and the airport runways, to deliver the computer-commanded groceries, all these and many more activities required an underclass of slaves or servants. But who was prepared to undertake such unherculean labours, when everybody had materially transcended class of any kind at all?

That was when the lottery was introduced. Lotteries based on money had long ago been abandoned out of lack of interest, but the rules of this lottery were staggeringly new and childishly simple. Each ticket cost fifteen minutes, and part of the lottery was that the purchaser had no control over the service that must be given during that short time - that depended entirely on the needs decided by the lottery committee, which of course was under the auspices of the government. So a person might be required to clean a street, or to attend an old age home and dispense kindness, or to hear children read in school, or to drive a construction wagon, or to plant flowers in the town park, or even to operate the stall that sold the lottery tickets. Each ticket cost fifteen minutes, and there was no limit to the number of tickets a purchaser might buy. Each week a number of prizes were awarded, corresponding to the number of tickets sold and the total number of hours which those tickets represented. If no one had the winning numbers, the prizes would be carried forward.

In the beginning, of course, everybody rushed to participate, simply because of the novelty of the thing - though it must be said that it damaged the government very badly when people discovered that the overcoming of human wants, which was the principal platform on which the government had won election, was so easily disproven by the onset of this new and seemingly insatiable desire. And it wasn't only novelty that people still desired - it was also time. The desire to have more time is infinite. In some cases, people were willingly buying ten or twelve or even fourteen hours' worth of tickets each day. Some found that they enjoyed the range and the variety of these "societal" activities so much, they were actually purchasing more tickets than there were hours in the day to fulfil their strict conditions.

That was when, for a brief experimental period, the reduction from fifteen to ten, and then from ten to just five minutes took place, which proved an even greater catastrophe for the system, for now everyone was rushing to buy an ever larger number of tickets, aware that the odds on winning were substantially increased while the possibility of actually fulfilling the tasks evaporated, because each ticket carried a different task and there simply wasn't enough time to get from one task to the other, let alone perform it. So the fifteen minutes were restored.

Instead, and somewhat insidiously, the organisers began to reduce the number of the tasks, even to localise them, so that one person buying forty or fifty tickets might well find themselves committed to ten or fifteen hours of unbroken grocery delivery or building work, unpaid and unrewarded except on the promissory note of unlimited time if you should be the lucky one who won (the media were full of tales of those who had won whole decades of time, such as the 108 year old woman who had been expected to die of lymphatic cancer more than twenty years before, but having won a roll-over lottery had had a full one million five hundred and twelve thousand minutes added to her life).

Those who have attacked all forms of lottery on moral grounds continue to insist that we will finish as a society riven once again by class, a society divided into mastery and slavery, into those who are satisfied with wealth and a short life and therefore do not buy the tickets, and those for whom there is no end of wanting, and who are literally enslaved to the lottery, prepared to work themselves to death for the half-chance of a longer life. But they are wrong, these Jeremiahs. Today, forty years since the introduction of the lottery, the novelty has long worn off and time itself begun to hang so heavily upon our over-satiated populace, that nobody at all will buy the tickets, except of course the old and the infirm, who understandably wish to acquire all the extra time they can, but who have anyway been excluded from the draw on the grounds that they are incapable of fulfilling the requirements of their fifteen minutes.

AN ARGUMENT

A scientist, a priest and a poet were arguing about which of them knew the true origins of the Universe, and which of them possessed the appropriate language to explain them.

"It's me," said the priest, "who knows that the beginning was God, as all things are God, and that God is Himself the Word with which I can explain the origin of all things."

"It's me," the scientist countered, "who has human reason and empiricism on his side. One may find the origins of the Universe by tracing life down to its smallest component parts, down to the atom, and through the neutron and the proton to the very nucleus of the atom, and down and still further down, to the ultimate and original monad, where you'll find a particle of such infinite minitude that it has no name and cannot be seen, but which may be described as an organism that is itself the Universe in microcosm."

Bowing his head, the poet acceded.

"It's certainly not me," he said, "who professes to knowing nothing about the origins of the Universe, and who uses language only to express the origins of his own uncertainty and ignorance and confusion. However, as both of you have adequately demonstrated, I am the closest, mine is the most appropriate, indeed the only apposite language. God and the particle indeed! In the beginning, it seems, was the metaphor."

DREAM-MURDER

That night, Simcha Hurlitz dreamed that he had killed a man. He saw the man's face in intense detail, as if through a microscope or the zoom lens of a camera: the eyes dilated by terror, the lips turned redder than their own redness by the blood that was mingling with his saliva. He saw the man's body, prone and prostrate on what could have been a mound of rock or flowers. He saw the dribble of blood trickling from beneath the man's clothing, though whether caused by sword or scimitar or some other weapon was unclear. He saw his own reflection, looming in the moonlight above the corpse, and though he didn't see the deed performed, he knew that it was he himself who was the murderer.

When he awoke, hours before dawn and in a febrid sweat, Simcha could remember every detail of the dream with grotesque clarity; but who the victim was - this he did not know. Yet he supposed the dream to have been authentic, the murder to have been genuine, the victim to have been, not a phantasm, but a previously real, a once flesh-and-blood, an erstwhile living man. For dreams are not films nor fictions, but the truths of the unconscious mind in its torpid state erupting into fleeting and fragmented yet still veracious images. So Simcha knew that he was guilty of the crime of murder. Though he had killed only in dream, still the unconscious is as much a part of a man as are his eye or mouth or heart, and what a man is capable of in sleep, surely he is no less capable of perpetrating when he's wide awake? How hard it is to accept such truths about oneself! Simcha felt in his heart a weight of guilt for his dream-crime that was almost too intense to bear. Yet what could he do?

For the guilt continued to oppress him, until gradually it began to destroy him, his life, his marriage. He became morose and taciturn. He tried to assuage his guilt in religion. But it didn't help. And at last guilt drove him to drink, left him sleeping on park benches or in the entrances to railway-stations. Until finally the police took him into their protection, the magistrate declared him a vagrant, the prison governor lectured him on the new life he was to begin leading as a punishment by society for his sins. But it was no good. He had killed in dream, and only in dream could he achieve absolution.

Then, one night, he had another dream. The same man appeared, and talked to him of the crime. Simcha was as astonished as he was terrified. He was hearing a story that was entirely new to him. The man talked about the civil war, about the generalissimo whom they had both befriended and who betrayed them exactly as they had both predicted. The man reminisced about a certain red-haired girl they had both loved in some small town in the back end of nowhere. He talked about Paris and Vienna, where they had travelled together. He talked and talked, until the dreamer learned the whole story of his victim's life and death. But still it remained unfamiliar to him. He didn't know this man, had never known him, would never know him. The man had clearly entered the wrong dream, the unconscious of the wrong dreamer. Yet Simcha felt immeasurable pity for the poor victim of his dream, who had died so suddenly, so unprepared, in such unexpected circumstances that he couldn't even find the right conscience to haunt and thereby give that death some meaning. As the man finished his tale at last, Simcha's eyes looked up through the darkness of sleep upon the bars on the window of his prison, and the sleeper knew that he had been absolved at last, by a man he didn't know, for a crime he hadn't even committed.

THE STATUE

The truth was, nobody had liked him. His arrogance, his womanising, his propensity towards the venal and the carnal, his atrocious table manners and his even more appalling taste in clothes, led the more kind-hearted to open hilarity at mention of his name, while others, firmer in their preparedness to pass judgements, declared the man a crank, a cad, an outrage and a charlatan, nonetheless continuing to invite him to their garden-parties and to attend those lectures that he gave to raise money for his expedition. The truth of this latter was that, in order to conduct the expedition at all, he had had to beg finances in a manner so toadying and sycophantic, the rich eventually gave him what he wanted, simply to be rid of him. The crew he gathered round him made mockery of motley, while the planning of the voyage, once it became rumoured, reduced the share values of his benefactors' companies by more than twenty-five per cent in just a day. Obituaries were being penned before the boat had even left the quay.

In the event however, luck was with him, far more than he deserved, and that he died a hero's death in the abject failure of his mission is something that must remain unsubstantiated, despite the oaths sworn by the three survivors, each one a proven liar and scoundrel - two of them ex-convicts and the third a convict-yet-to-be - that he had personally witnessed what, given the remaining details of the story of their miraculous escape, must be taken with a very large wave of sea-salt. Yet such a death, such witnesses, are the staple of immortality.

This very afternoon, we unveiled at last his statue, a triumph of Carrera marble even if the artefact might not be truly verisimilitudinous of the original. Thousands gathered for the ceremonial unveiling, rich and poor, benefactors and critics, admirers and detractors. The truth was, he had become a statue long ago, and it had never really mattered whether his expedition reached its goal or not, for frankly very few understood the significance of that esoteric purpose, and what matters is the rarity of setting out and not the uniqueness of arriving. He had been a statue even when he was still a man, and what was miscarved on the marble, what was raised on the damaged plinth - a workman had stumbled while putting it in place and a piece of the pedestal had come loose on one side - was simply the human need to perch something of significance upon a column, and to know that, in some small and yet imaginably important way, one had oneself contributed.

RACHEL

This morning I happened to pass through the western quarter of the town and remembered the old woman, Rachel. She lives, as she has lived for fifty years now, in a ramshackle dwelling on the perimeter of the council estate, a hut that would have been torn down long ago had it not been for the compassion or negligence of some petty functionary. Little is known of her except by rumour; and that only by those few who, like myself, have come to learn of her existence.

It's said that she was orphaned at the age of five and brought up by a series of foster parents who quickly changed their minds about adopting. At sixteen she was married, at seventeen a widow; at the age of eighteen she locked herself away in what was then a woodman's hut, and has never to my knowledge emerged since. For all the world she's been dead these fifty years. Progress and two world wars, even the residents of the council estate, have passed her by, oblivious of or indifferent to her existence. Never has she given or received anything. Alone, ignored, she paces the boards of a run-down shack, living on berries that she grows in flower-pots and the rain-water that seeps through the cracks in the roof, an old woman waiting to die.

Remembering her, I couldn't help but wonder why such a woman had ever been born, what place she could possibly have in the universal scheme, what malign god could have imposed such a fate on her, what sin she could have committed that life should punish her in this way. Now, in the quiet of evening, it has come to me that, though she lives and will die alone, though she will leave behind no will or testament, no soul to mourn, one simple act that requires nothing of her and takes nothing from her may fulfil and justify her life. Now, in the dark, still night, it has come to me that I am her destiny, that she lives and will die only that her name might be given to this poem, that her spirit may find rest within these lines, and its writing breed unforgetfulness.

URGE AND DEMIURGE

"He saw a ladder, whose top reached the heavens"

Music is the most human of the arts, closest to reason, rooted in mathematical logic, synthesised out of the pure abstraction of symbols. Poetry extends this back towards paganism, by adding significance to symbol and adhering to the elemental in nature. Literature is pure paganism, the devaluation of both symbol and nature into mythology, the substitution of intellect by imagination. Drama is pure myth, the imitation of nature. Painting is a retreat still further into the primitive, depiction of nature in its most pristine form. Dance is a liberation from the human, allowing the body to become an aspect of nature itself. The last phase is sculpture, which simply remoulds nature, making of it its own symbol, matter abstracted from itself, fixed in its own elements. From here it isn't difficult to imagine the divinity, working with rocks and boulders, trying to breathe life into inanimate objects.

ESAU'S VERSION

When my father was a boy, his father took him on a long and foolish journey, he and two other lads of similar age. The journey nearly killed all four of them; it did kill my mother - not to mention a poor and helpless ram. But father survived, and lived to a ripe old age, and if not entirely comfortable, then to what might best be called a guilt-edged security. His life was mostly spent trying to maintain grandfather's wells, a business that cost him not a few arguments, and most of grandfather's immense wealth and power, and which left him in old age blind and bed-ridden. He was a fairly insignificant man, my father, a patriarch by birth though not by temperament, who would have died unremembered in history had he been any other father's son, any other half-brother's half-brother, had he himself not fathered my brother Jacob and myself. He died almost bankrupt: my grandfather's estate in tatters except for a handful of sand-filled, empty wells; and some superstition about a secret covenant for which the lawyers could find absolutely no evidence in writing.

Yet this was not his only legacy. For he left behind, archetype of archetypes, the story of his near death, of that long and foolish journey of immense insignificance, for the rest of us to chew on like a cow the cud. Any more than the dried-out wells, I never wanted that legacy, though it was my birthright. It was too heavy - far heavier than the mere sticks of wood that father had carried. By the time they reached me, those sticks had become a cross - why should I carry that cross? No, in truth, I'm grateful to Jacob for wanting to bear that burden, for agreeing to take it from my shoulders. What kind of a birthright was it anyway, what kind of a legacy to inflict upon a child? No, I sold my burden for a mess of potage. But truthfully, I didn't need the potage.

THE CONFLAGRATION

A story by Borges - at least the second greatest writer of the twentieth century - begins as follows:

"One of Hawthorne's parables which was almost masterly, but not quite, because a preoccupation with ethics mars it, is "Earth's Holocaust". In that allegorical story Hawthorne foresees a moment when men, satiated by useless accumulations, resolve to destroy the past. They congregate at evening on one of the vast western plains of America to accomplish the feat. Men come from all over the world. They make a gigantic bonfire kindled with all the genealogies, all the diplomas, all the medals, all the orders, all the judgements, all the coats of arms, all the crowns, all the sceptres, all the tiaras, all the purple robes of royalty, all the canopies, all the thrones, all the spiritous liquors, all the bags of coffee, all the boxes of tea, all the cigars, all the love letters, all the artillery, all the swords, all the flags, all the martial drums, all the instruments of torture, all the guillotines, all the gallows trees, all the precious metals, all the money, all the titles of property, all the constitutions and codes of law, all the books, all the mitres, all the vestments, all the sacred writings that potulate and fatigue the Earth. Hawthorne views the conflagration with astonishment and even shock..."

And so he should, for these men have gathered to build the great funeral pyre of History, which will destroy the past once and for all (as Li Shu, the First Chinese Emperor, tried previously to do). But in the event, so large was the fire, so black was its smoke, so wide was its renown, so profound was its significance, that in trying to destroy the past these men had in fact created it absolutely and for ever.

THE KNIGHT'S STORY

Because of Don Miguel and his childlike imagination - his tilting at the windmills of literature - all the world today believes that the Quixote was, yes a comic figure, but essentially a gentle, honest, good, well-meaning man, whose failing virtue was simply that he dreamed beyond his stature and aspired to heights of human chivalry that he couldn't possibly hope to scale. Supreme faults! Laudatory vices! Immaculate failures! Who more noble than the Quixote - unless perhaps Don Miguel himself, for imagining him?

But it was, truly, imagination. I, Don Pedro de la Santa Milanerva, I alone know the truth, I alone knew the real Quixote - the one who raped the twelve year old Dulcinea Castillano and robbed the house of Don Sancho Panza - a bad, a wicked, a truly evil man, no fool either, but a cruel schemer, who drank, and whored, and stole, stole even from the very poorest and from the whores that he himself had bought.

I knew him, and once I might have killed him and been thanked for it, when I came upon him in the barn of my own villa, forcing his will at knife-point on a serving-girl. But I didn't kill him. The young Miguel and the by-then middle-aged Quixote were both guests in my house, and I knew the Quixote, but I knew the young Miguel much better, a mere boy still, but with an imagination of extraordinary fecundity, one that bent towards goodness quite as keenly as the Quixote's bent towards licentiousness. I let the Quixote live, allowed him a further month in my house to seduce the young Miguel's imagination with half-truths and concocted tales, or tales from which he had stripped the vilest details like a highway corpse. Would the world really have thanked me for killing him? No, it would have been better to kill the serving-girl, to stop her doing what eventually she did - inform the magistrate of what the Quixote had done to her. So he was condemned to die, and his body ascended into the ephemeral fire, and his soul descended into the eternal one; but by then it no longer mattered. Already my young protégé was practicing his craft, already his imagination had begun to reinvent, already his pen had begun to weave its magical fables; already the authentic Don Quixote was being supplanted by the mythical one. No, I was right not to interfere when I came upon him in that act of sin. Much more than that - for in that moment of not killing an evil man, did I not, myself, give birth to a truly saintly one?

CHRONICLE OF A DREAM

Vision in dream is patterned like time in memory, random and fragmentary, isolating incidents like objects seen through a cobweb or an image reflected in a sheet of breaking glass...

I remember dreaming the pale light of a star that reached me a million years after the star burned out, and the darkness which the light accentuated, and the skyscape which stretched into oblivion.

I remember dreaming the dry, silent stalks of grass, distended over dilapidated coffins, withering into their own pale winters, above the farm where Menelaus was buried, and where a man named Bellafiore will one day unearth his rusted sword.

I remember dreaming the cedars of Tyre, their roots rotten with dried leaves, their trunks heavy with unspeakable fossils, which I would later transport through time and space and set below the imaginary village of my novel.

I remember dreaming the long, slow river, at once Jordan and Euphrates, flowing darker than blood, endless as human suffering - the teeming river of History.

I remember dreaming the eternal sand that lay buried in the sea's hourglass, and it was the same sand that Proust sifted, the same sand whose riddles Moses read.

I remember dreaming, and finally I remember dreaming a single, solitary man, who stood in the centre of this oblique labyrinth, bearded and manifold, ageless, standing now upon the steep, undaunted bank, firm as any rock, relentless as a summer drought, stumbling now towards some wild, lucid uncertainty - Whitman the chronicler, who published the sad statistics of this aimless, rootless world, who imagined that he was this gaunt, proud universe, and wrote its autobiography.

SOLOMON

It is said that no man of his time was wiser than King Solomon - he who built the Jewish Temple, that oblique labyrinth whose Holy of Holies contained the infinity of time and space and the key to the mysteries of the Universe - and that this wisdom was the result of his gifts of fortune-telling and clairvoyance, his ability to decipher those obscure hieroglyphs which record the deeds of the future.

At the age of sixty-five - the Bible, which is lunary, and generally perverse in these matters, gives an hundred and eleven - grown tired of meagre prophecies and the transparency of political affairs, he set himself the task of creating a work of literature. This would eventually lead to the exquisite "Song Of Songs" and the no less remarkable "Book Of Common Maxims" which is also called "The Book Of Proverbs". It is believed that he also produced a third masterpiece - some say a version of the Bible itself - but the manuscript of this latter has, alas, been lost.

Among the documents pertaining to Eliezer ben Avraham, Solomon's Chief Secretary, was found the following missive, set down not in Canaanitic but in Hebrew, the royal tongue, and consequently attributable to the King. The missive reads as follows:-

"The actual process of creative writing is surprisingly straight-forward, a question of finding a suitable starting-point and then selecting one from an infinite range of possible developments. For my own work I have decided to begin with the somewhat contentious statement that 'all happy families are alike, but an unhappy family is unhappy in its own way'. Having stated this I am, as I have said, left with any number of possible developments. However, since all things are predetermined and thus foreseeable, I have been forced to choose one way and to reject, among all others, one in particular. The one I have chosen was forced on me by History, God, and the experiences of my own life, the unhappy family of my book being, of course, that of the children of Israel. The one I have rejected - the one I would have chosen above all others had I been free to choose - was taken from me by chance, fate, and the hand of time, for in deciphering the hieroglyphs I have found that book already written, telling of another family's unhappiness, beginning with the self-same phrase, which a man named Tolstoi (יותשלוט) will one day call 'Anna Karenina'" (הנינרק אינא).

THE LIBRARY AT BABEL

We did not intend to build this library. Our aim was greater than that. Our aim was to construct the Tower of Babel. But God intervened. He confused our language, so we could not communicate the plans for the Tower. A meeting was convened, to discuss what should be done, but none of us could understand the proposals, and so, by the tacit agreement of silence, the Tower was abandoned.

Unaware that I was not alone in this endeavour, I set out to create a perfect language (this is not it), one with which God could not interfere, one which would restore our powers of communication and thus enable us to resume the project. It has taken many years, but already there are several of us who have understood the basic problems. Between us we have gathered copies of all the books that exist, and have written countless more ourselves. That is why we built this library, which, as you can see, is so vast that it will soon reach the very gates of Heaven.

LITERARY GENEALOGIES

In my novel "Going To The Wall", I recorded the details of a remarkable literary genealogy, and wondered whether it might infer a new approach to literary criticism. Here - with some slight adaptation to make it coherent out of context - is what I wrote:

Osip Mandelstam's satire on Stalin, which would lead to his exile and death, was written and recited in the apartment of Boris Pasternak, sometime in 1934. Exactly forty years earlier, the infant Pasternak was living in his father's official residence as the Director of Art of the College of Arts in Moscow, in Myasnitskaya, opposite the main Post Office. The apartment, as Pasternak records in "An Essay In Autobiography", was "in an annexe across the yard, separate from the main building...From the balcony the inhabitants of the building watched the ceremony of transferring the remains of the Emperor Alexander III in 1894, and two years later a part of the festivities in honour of the coronation of Nicholas II."

In 1944, Pasternak tells us, he read the following under the heading "1894", on page 125 of a recent Soviet book, "Moscow in the Life and Work of Leo Tolstoy", by N.S. Rodionov:

"'On 23 November, Tolstoy and his daughters went to a concert given at the flat of the painter Leonid Pasternak, Director of the College of Arts. The musicians were Pasternak's wife, the cellist Brandukov and the violinist Grzhimaldi, both Professors at the Conservatoire."

Tolstoy himself records this visit in one of his letters, informing his correspondent that the music he heard that evening was Tchaikovsky's "Trio". 1894, incidentally, was the year in which Tchaikovsky died, as that same winter did the great Anton Rubinstein, whose brother Nikolai founded the Conservatoire where Leonid's friends were Professors, and where Boris would study music with Scriabin before deciding to make poetry his career. Pasternak's "Essay In Autobiography" is translated into English by Manya Harari, who just happens to be the mother-in-law of the English poet Craig Raine; and it was Raine who, in his capacity as editor of poetry for Faber & Faber, brought out the only English collection to date of the poems of Osip Mandelstam...

I could, in fact, have gone much further. Another former editor at Faber's, Martin Bradbrook, later founded his own music publishing house, which brought out, among others, the cello works of Brandukov and the short series of teaching pieces for violin by Grzhimaldi. Rodionov, the critic of Tolstoy, also wrote an infamous attack on Solzhenitsyn, which was instrumental in securing that writer's exile, and of course Solzhenitsyn completes the circle, because he was the very first, in his Gulag Archipelago, to record the precise details of the sufferings of those "zeks" of whom none was ever more famous in fact than Mandelstam and in fiction than Pasternak's "Dr Zhivago". Solzhenitsyn's English agent...but one could go on forever, making these fascinating connections.

How would this new style of literary criticism work? For one thing, since literature is the subject, an element of fiction might be introduced (I have done precisely that in the preceding paragraphs), and in addition one might include the significant meetings that did not take place (the one between Anthony and Octavius before Actium comes to mind), the longed-for meetings (such as Henry James' famous dream of telling Mark Twain to his face just what he really thought of him), the fantasy-meetings (I'm thinking of those splendid lines of Oswald Cuthbertson's:

> "If I could take my dinner with the greats
> a cigar with Bleistein, say, or talking love with Yeats
> or sit awhile discussing plans and tactics
> with Napoleon in a Petersburg café, or semantics
> with Wordsworth, or share a wafer with St Paul
> or drink a toast to Spanish wine with Charles de Gaulle")

or even the more mystical meetings, like seeing Coleridge's flower in a dream and finding it in your hand upon awakening, or Moses' encounter with Jehovah on the holy mountain.

Another good example might be that of Conor Cruise O'Brien, the Irish statesman and former editor of The Times, whose father signed the paper that overthrew Parnell, whose mother was the model for Joyce's revolutionary heroine in one of his "Dubliners" tales, and whose drinking-friend Malachi McCourt (a name that surely owes a precursive debt to Samuel Beckett) was the brother of that Frank McCourt who half a century later would write the splendid "Angela's Ashes". While Professor of English at Columbia, O'Brien was responsible for recruiting, inter alia, both the poet E.E. Thompson and the critic George Steiner...

May I request that someone, anyone, who inhabits the hells of either New York or the afterlife - these two may well be the same place - and might happen to encounter someone who has met, or otherwise find occasion to ask of Harold Bloom (no relation to Leopold, so far as I'm aware) or Queenie Leavis (no point asking old F.R - his wife always wore the trousers in that family), whether they know of anyone else who may at some time have considered - even perhaps rejected - this approach.

THE EAGLES

In the scheme of the gods, nothing is unforeseeable, nothing is without reason, nothing is fallible, nothing is uncorrectible, no event is too unlikely that contingencies do not exist, no incident is so complete that it cannot be rescinded, no cause but has its effect and each effect its cause; for everything participates in the scheme of Creation.

Thus, for example, there was the great plan of the gods to rid the Caucasus of a species of locust that was threatening to destroy the region. The locusts had themselves been introduced into the Caucasus to get rid of a particular strain of wheat whose need for water was more than the region could sustain (the wheat had originally been planted to help drain the marshes created by winter flooding at the source of the river, flooding itself caused by the melting of the ice-cap due to... and so forth, along the tracks of evolution, to the initial scheme of Creation itself.)

Once the last of the wheat had been consumed, it was necessary to eliminate the locusts. To do this the gods sent eagles to the Caucasus; the eagles favoured the locusts because of the remarkable quality of their livers, which had been hugely enriched by wheat and water. The eagles devoured the locusts; but then, for want of food, began to seek it elsewhere. So the eagles had, in their turn, to be removed; to do this the gods allowed Prometheus to steal the secret of fire, and Prometheus used the fire to burn down the trees in which the eagles roosted; but he couldn't destroy the eagles themselves.

Now, in the great deforested desert of the Caucasus, the scheme of Creation has come almost to a standstill. Virtually no man nor woman inhabits this dead region, practically no bird flies there nor creature dwells among its unwelcoming wastes, almost no plants or flowers grow in that infertile soil. Only there remains the secret of the fire, which Prometheus refuses to surrender, still burning among dead shrubs and in the ashes and the cinders of the trees. And there remains the problem of the homeless, hungry eagles, with their insatiable appetite for liver.

VERONA 1634

There was a feud between the Capulets and the Montagues. I had made my way from the ghetto to a small hotel above the shop of an apothecary, and taken up my lodgings there. On the day that Paris was killed I was visited by a young friar, who asked me if I would deliver a letter on his behalf, a letter which, he maintained, could save the lives of one member of each of the feuding houses. I made him a glass of jasmine tea, and we sat together some several hours discussing the sacred texts of the Cabbala and the Pauline Church, the pessimism of whose metaphysics are so similar. It was in the course of this discussion that we concluded that the letter was of no importance, since even if we saved the two young lovers now, the laws of nature are such that both were doomed eventually to die anyway - and then we burned the letter. Thus we did not save the lives of the young lovers, but we did, in our small way, contribute to the writing of an immortal play, which popular folklore would elevate far above the deaths of those two mere mortals.

Some months later two statues were erected in the town square, depicting the young lovers, symbolising the reconciliation of the two great houses (who were wiped out by plague some eleven years later), but the statues have now been demolished by the heirs of Paris, who took command of the town last month. Undoubtedly the most alarming consequence of the coup is the fact that, while no mention has yet been made of that play to which we contributed, the new government, in the name of the Protestant Reformation, has ordered the burning of all the sacred texts of the Cabbala and the Pauline Church, an edict whose execution I hope - but against hope - to avert through the publication of this letter.

THE ANGEL

In "The Book of Origins" (usually known by its Greek misnomer, "The Book of Genesis") it is recorded that Jacob, returning home after fourteen years in exile, was scared to face his brother Esau, rightly fearing that Esau would still bear a grudge against him for the birthright that Jacob had twice stolen. On the night before his arrival he sent a half of his possessions on ahead as a gift for his brother, hoping in this way to temper Esau's wrath. Yet he remained scared. He prayed to the Almighty, asking God to give him the strength he needed, and God sent one of His angels to wrestle with Jacob; and though the angel cheated by touching the hollow of Jacob's thigh and putting it out of joint, still it was Jacob who prevailed, and received the angel's blessing, and became Israel.

This is all that "The Book of Origins" tells us about the wrestling-match. We know who the protagonists were. We know that an amicable reunion with Esau is implied. We know that the Almighty does not bestow favours or intervene personally. We know that by wrestling Jacob overcame his own frailty and discovered the strength of his own being. We know that, on the mythological level, we are secretly witnessing the rite of the initiation of Jacob as the Sacred King of Israel. We know that the incident is intended as a parable, and that nothing in parable is without significance. We know that Jacob's adversary was an angel of the Almighty; but what we do not know is this:

Why, out of an infinity of angels, did the Almighty choose this one in particular to wrestle with Israel at Penuel?

SECOND-IN-COMMAND

When the great national revolution came to an end at last, after more than seventeen years of unbroken war, Colonel Rodrigo, second-in-command of the victorious Marxist Liberation Front, thanked his friend and leader Colonel Ramirez (in that army of social egalitarians there was only one rank, that of Colonel, which all men held, from the leader to the cook), and told him he would not accept the post of Minister of Justice which he had been offered in the new regime. The decision was surprising, for Colonel Rodrigo had a strong affection for Justice (indeed, his reason for declining the post illustrated this affection perfectly), and no one had fought more heroically in its name than he - unless, it goes without saying, Colonel Ramirez himself.

"If I become Minister of Justice," Colonel Rodrigo told his friend, sitting together at dinner in the recently renamed People's Palace, "I will face three choices: to become a failure, or a criminal, or a corpse. That's to say, I can try to enact justice according to the needs of the government and this new, young state of illiterate peasants and incompetent coolies, in which case I'll fail to bring justice at all, though I may well succeed in bringing economic growth and political stability. Or I can fail by not trying to bring justice at all but simply becoming an oppressor, who takes advantage of his office to become wealthy and corrupt and libertine, a bastard just (or rather unjust) like all the bastards we've just (and justly) kicked out. Thirdly, I can enact perfect justice for all men equally, in which case I'll become a hero of the revolution, and as such a threat to your undisputed leadership - so you'll be forced to have me killed. Therefore I shall take the only way-out that's available to a second-in-command."

The Colonel smiled and continued. "'All revolutions are doomed to failure. The first generation, the pioneering one, is followed by that of the opportunists. The third continues the first out of habit; the fourth out of inertia. Eventually the movement turns its battle inwards, splitting into factions, groups, sects, one against the other, one against all. Substance gives way to superficiality. Personalities replace ideas; slogans replace ideals. The lofty goals are lost; the message is forgotten. Now the struggle revolves around titles and positions. The process is predictable, ineluctable.' These aren't my words, but those of Elie Wiesel, speaking of the Hasidic movement in northern Europe. Nonetheless, they're apposite. I shall take to the hills and fight for the true revolution. I give you five years. Make the revolution succeed or I will take up the fight against you, and kill you if I can or if you don't kill me first."

Colonel Ramirez ground his teeth, and chewed, as was his custom, on the end of a matchstick.

"I should have killed you," he said, "when I had the chance, all those years ago, at the Battle of Las Palmas."

"There would have been another to take my place."

"I should have killed him too."

"And then another. Do you not know that it's the fate of all leaders to be vanquished, not by their enemies, but by their closest friends?"

In sadness the two men parted, never to meet again. That same night Colonel Rodrigo suffered a particularly painful bout of dysentery, which caused his stomach to bleed and lacerated the scar tissue of an ancient belly-wound. He was buried with full military and civil honours in the recently renamed Cemetery of the Martyrs.

THE CLERK MACBETH

I don't like to speak ill of someone who only began working for us this week; yet there's no doubt that all of us, without exception, have noticed something quirky, something very slightly disturbing, something positively peculiar in the manner of the new clerk, Macbeth. Nor is it simply his arrogance, his high-and-mighty attitude, his way of speaking to you as if he and he alone knows what's best for the company. No, it's far more than that. Yesterday, for example, at lunchtime, who could help but be surprised by the glee and the enthusiasm with which he accepted Miss Davies' playful suggestion that she read his horoscope out of the newspaper; or shocked when Mrs Bailey took from her bag a mirror, for no other purpose than to arrange her hair and put on her lipstick before going home, to see him rush over and seize the mirror from her hands, hurl it crashing to the floor in an uncontrollable rage. Such behaviour would be inexcusable at the best of times, and even a member of the Board could hardly expect to get away with it; but from one so new in his post it was positively outrageous, and I was quite honestly tempted to go and speak to Mr Duncan, the Branch Manager, about it. But then, this morning, when he'd supposedly gone down to the basement to archive some old files, I actually saw him, pacing the corridor outside the Branch Manager's office, talking to himself out loud, gazing into his open hand as though he were imagining it held a knife.

A PARADOX

"What are we supposed to do?" the policeman wondered. "The newspapers want us to be heroes; the Radicals want us to disappear altogether; the Church wants us to clamp down ever more stringently; the Liberals complain about our methods; the Judges say we overwork them; the prison governors claim the cells are overcrowded; the Conservatives insist the streets are dangerous for law-abiding citizens. Everyone wants something different from us. How are we supposed to do our job properly and still keep everybody happy?"

"Ah yes," replied the lawyer, "but if everybody was happy, then we wouldn't have a job to do."

THE MIRROR AND THE MAZE

Were Borges to have imagined a mirror which was also a maze (and somewhere, no doubt, he did indeed do so), it would surely have been the sort of mirror in which a man's reflection showed him, not who he was, but who he dreamed of being. Thus, in the mirror, Hitler saw the image and the likeness of Napoleon, who had himself encountered the image and the likeness of Genghis Khan, who had...Similarly, seeking His chimera in the shadow of as-yet-uncreated glass, God looked into the Chaos and saw the image and the likeness of that creature He would call Man. For myself, I imagine a monster named Posterity, peering into the rose-coloured glass of the mirror of literature, and imagining it sees the image and the likeness of a fabulous, mythic beast, a literary unicorn. And the name of this impossible creature who never was (unless, perhaps, in the realm of dreams) will be Borges.

And if Borges himself were to look into the mirror, if Borges himself were to describe the mythic creature at the centre of the maze, I imagine he would bear a distinct resemblance to Poe, to Berkeley, perhaps to Valéry, certainly to Kafka; but mostly to the twenty-fourth century Japanese poet Akaido Mishigami, of whom a certain literary critic of some considerable stature will one day write that "an artist always creates his own precursors, and Mishigami's, by his own admission, was Borges".

THE TWO SONS OF GOD

It is generally held that the Almighty had not one but two sons. In the Talmud we read that Adam, the first son, was thirty-three years old when he was born; in the Gospels that Joshua Bar Joseph, the second son, was thirty-three years old when he was crucified. From the former we learn that Man fell from grace because he ate of the fruit of the tree of knowledge; from the latter that the knowledge of grace was given back to Man when he was hung from the tree of Calvary like a rotten fruit. Because the two stories are related separately, and because the two incidents are held to have happened several thousand years apart, it is presumed that there were two sons of God, in different places and at different times. Yet a myth is a universal phenomenon, and as such it does not exist in place or time, but simultaneously in all places and at all times. The true account is therefore quite different.

There was only one son of God, and he was the son of God by a mortal woman. At the age of thirty-three he was crucified on the tree of Calvary, that men might know the greatness of God, and come into His Kingdom. By means of a final miracle the body of the dead man was transformed into a fruit on that tree, which now (of course) stood at the centre of that Paradise he had promised, while the spirit of the dead man was resurrected, and given the name Adam (which means Man and Earth), and this Adam plucked the fruit of his own death from the tree, that men might obtain final and absolute knowledge of all things, good and evil.

This formula is preferable for two reasons. Firstly it teaches us that grace and sin are merely two sides of the same syllogism, that death is merely the process of transition from life to life, that a man may gain and lose Paradise in a single moment. Secondly it clears up a mystery that theologians have wrestled with for millennia, namely: we know who was the mortal woman who gave birth to Joshua, but who was the mortal woman who gave birth to Adam?

RETURN JOURNEY

"So ended my ten years of isolation in the country"

Two boys were sitting on the station wall, playing cards for marbles. A man in a Basque beret was reading a newspaper, whose headline told of the death of Charles de Gaulle. A girl stood on the pavement, clutching a parcel to her breast. A fruit-seller squatted beside his barrow, gazing at the posters on the cinema wall. Through the windows of a café I could see two men drinking cassis; from time to time the waiter would cross towards them and whisper something at which all three would laugh. From the steps that led down to the Metro came a never-ending file of people, who passed into the falling evening as unobtrusively as the innumerable cars and buses, rendered anonymous by streetlight. Not a face turned to look at another face, not an ear turned to listen nor a voice to speak. Under the bleak shadows of moon and neon, beyond the station and the steps, the crowd jostled frenetically past me. I lingered on the steps a while, then turned towards the city, making my own way through the busy streets, gladly resuming what already seemed my long-lost privacy.

THE COVENANT

The god who lived at the summit of Mt Sinai had waited centuries for somebody to take up the burden of the Law he had conceived. Few people lived in or passed through that desert: the occasional nomadic tribe who frankly had no use for legal codes; the occasional marauding band of warriors who had nothing but contempt for any law; the occasional king or priest or prophet who were so puffed up with their own self-conceited opinions that no one else's laws were of the slightest interest; the occasional guerrilla band crossing the desert to or from another freedom struggle - whether against left or right-wing, legal or illegal despotism - who were so committed to their own ideology that they wouldn't hear nor heed another. And then, at last, the Hebrews came fleeing out of Egypt, a forlorn rabble, slaves and beggars for the most part, an occasional whore, an Egyptian prince named Moses disguised as an Israelite - and since this Moses needed a law (and frankly none other was available), and since this god needed a people (and certainly none other was available), God and Moses met on the summit of Mt Sinai and struck their bargain.

THE WALL OF THE BARBARIANS

"All art and construction are vanity. Look to the culture of the plants and trees and fishes." (Emperor Liang Tchu)

The Emperor Liang Tchu ordered the construction of a wall around the whole length of his kingdom - a kingdom not so vast as China, yet large enough. It was to be no ordinary wall however, for he was no ordinary emperor. Unlike that barbarian monstrosity, the Great Wall of China, this would not serve simply as a protecting fence and a boundary marker. No, this was to be the Great Wall of Culture - for the Emperor conceived of his kingdom as a garden, and his reign as the nurturing of that magnificent flower Civilisation, and his divine duty to re-establish, if it were possible, the original Garden of Happiness and Innocence, where Harmony was the first and only principle, and where the fruits of all trees could be eaten with impunity.

So the Emperor sent out his armies to the north and south and east and west, and wherever they went they pillaged and spoiled and desecrated - or, rather, they mercifully tore down the dreadful and futile Towers of Babel of the philistines, and left in their places only the rubble of spring flowers and the debris of newly-planted woods.

Their mission required many years (and over the years many wars, and in the wars many deaths), but at last they had collected sufficient "bricks", and the "gardeners" - as the Emperor liked to call them - could begin their work. Thus was the Great Wall and the Great Garden of Culture built: one set of bricks taken from the Louvre and another from the Hermitage, one from the Coliseum and another from the cathedral at Bologna, one from the Palace of Westminster and another from the Hanging Gardens at Babylon - one, in short, from every temple of unculture the barbarians had ever built.

Today, visitors are welcome to peruse the Emperor's magnificent gardens, the treasure-house of his people, where every flower and fish and bird and creature known to Man lives in the harmony of the Emperor's sublime creation. An entire lily-pond built of bricks that were once the Elysée Palace. Fountains serviced by pumps that formerly maintained the Volga Dam. The perfectly reconstructed gardens of the Alhambra. The remarkable rockery whose centrepiece is the Black Rock of Mecca. A marvellous dyke to irrigate the paddy-fields, built out of pyramid-stones. The great vine-trellises that were once the pillars of the Acropolis. Flower-beds pebbled with the splintered fragments of the Lincoln Memorial. Terraced hillsides that could have been the natural amphitheatres of the

Mayan Indians. Pergolas ornamented with gold leaf melted from the dome of St Peter's. And more, much more. But mostly visitors come to see the great wall itself that surrounds the gardens, the Great Wall of Culture as it's called by some, the Wall of the Barbarians as it's known by others.

THE OBJECT

In a dream he saw an object that amazed him. In shape it was indescribable, an object of indefinite size that contained all possibilities, the seeds of all life, all knowledge, an object from which nothing could be excluded. Looking upon that object he knew that it was ineffable, inexorable, the ultimate form, and he wondered if he had not, perhaps, been granted a vision of the deity, or a glimpse of the unity of galaxies that comprise the universe - but looking again he recognised that it was neither of these, for the object was neither so large nor so small.

Re-entering the dream the object reappeared, and he understood that the object was itself his dream, and that in dreaming he was seeing the object from the inside. For the dream of the object was the object of the dream, and the mind settled upon its own darkness, and the vision sank beneath its own unutterable lucidity.

THE PARADOX OF THE LAW

Besides the six hundred and thirteen unchallengeable statutes and commandments handed down by the legislator Moses, the majority of our laws are not written down but based on tradition, and the most important of our traditions is the perennial reinterpretation of the laws; since this tradition has remained unchallenged for more than three millennia already, it has itself acquired the status of a law, and consequently there is nobody today who would dare to question even the smallest fragment of it.

THE MAN IN THE BOWLER HAT

The man in the bowler hat sips tea while reading his Daily Telegraph. His passive face reveals none of the scars of his experiences, but these can easily be guessed: a gash above one eye from a piece of shrapnel or displaced fuselage; a weal on the scalp from the falling motion of a Prussian rifle; the memory of a stolen kiss, pressing upon his conscience like a bruise. These are not things he talks about; they live on in the annals of memory, curios to be examined in later years when nostalgia and grandchildren encourage his self-esteem. His hand doesn't tremble as he reads, nor is there a single word that can shock or surprise him. He's seen it all with his own eyes, has lived through the very worst, has done his duty to himself, his family, his country, and now he reaps his just rewards, preparing himself for that long retirement when, if he has time, he will learn in detail the lessons of experience. The man in the bowler hat is a survivor. He knows what is right, for he has fought to defend it. He knows what is good, for he has tasted it on his own tongue. He knows what men are capable of, for he has witnessed it. What he does not know is that we are watching him. What he does not know is that secret part of each of us that would like to plunge a knife into his heart.

MOSES

It is said of Moses that, despite overcoming his stutter, despite acquiring the skills of a magician, and an orator, and a soldier, and a lawyer, despite meeting the Almighty face to face and surviving the encounter, despite all his life's achievements - more, perhaps, than any man who ever lived - still he was prohibited from entering the Promised Land, because of a single sin he had committed, and his name was excised from the legend of the Exodus, and - though this isn't stated but merely inferred - he surrendered any hope of being taken up to Heaven when he died.

Yet perhaps he didn't die; perhaps immortality was his punishment and his fate; perhaps he's still sitting there, on the summit of his desert mountain, outside the Promised Land, outside the gates of Heaven, on the very border of History, at the very edge of the wilderness of eternity, encouraging those who lack his will or obduracy, urging them across the threshold.

THE MYTHIC BEAST

Antonio Pigafetta, a Florentine navigator who went with Magellan on the first voyage around the world, wrote, upon his passage through the southern lands of America, a strictly accurate account that nonetheless resembles a venture into fantasy.

In it, he recorded that he had seen hogs with navels on their haunches, clawless birds whose hens laid eggs on the backs of their mates, and others still, resembling tongueless pelicans, with beaks like spoons. He wrote of having seen a misbegotten creature with the head and ears of a mule, a camel's body, the legs of a deer and the whinny of a horse. He described how the first native encountered in Patagonia was confronted with a mirror, whereupon that impassioned giant lost his senses to the terror of his own image.

What Pigafetta did not describe - and could not have been expected to describe, since it existed at this time only as phantasy and possibility and not yet as reality; only existed, that is, as cause, but not yet as effect - was this: a surly-looking, short, squat creature with a moustache like a strip of potato peel over full, sensuous lips; eyes made out of celluloid and painted the colour of kodachrome; with a golden pen in its breast pocket reputedly the gift of Castro; and a number of iguana tails caught up in the strands of its hair, but using hair for their disguise. Pigafetta also failed to notice that, when this creature spoke, it used only the words of its hundred year old grandmother, who had died anyway some thirty-three years previously; that when this creature looked, it did so out of seventy million eyes; that when it slept - which it rarely did for it was so hungry - it dreamed not of food nor even of sleep, but only of entering the dream in which it was itself created, in order to unmake that dream and be reborn as someone else; that when it cried - which it did incessantly - it produced a wild, shrieking howl of pain, scarcely distinguishable from laughter; and that when it laughed - which it had never been known to do except in strictest privacy - whole governments were capable of being smothered in the fall-out.

Pigafetta also failed to observe the idolatry paid to this creature by the entire continent of South America, which had given to it the status of a god scarcely less than that afforded to Quetzalcoatl himself; and now imagined this creature as another incarnation of the mythical Phoenix or plumed serpent - a bird that Pigafetta never saw, but which would not have surprised him - and upon whose every utterance the people of that entire continent hung, as though he were both Moses and the backside of God and the very mountain on which and the cloud of fire in which those two fantastic and implausible beings had met.

It is said of this creature that, when it speaks, whole villages are cured of centuries of insomnia and rush to board locomotives that will speed them into the twenty-first century. Anthropologists witnessing the creature's utterances have recorded consequent phenomena of both cataclysmic and apocalyptic varieties, amongst them: the instantaneous convening of summit meetings by Prime Ministers and Heads of State, whose very positions of authority may now have been completely undermined; volcanic eruptions and the flooding of previously desert regions by secret, underground springs; the recovered sexual virility of an eighty-six year old man; seven pleas for clemency by convicted bandits simultaneously granted in seven different countries by seven political leaders of seven different ideological persuasions whose one and only similarity was that they had never previously granted any pleas for clemency at all; the apparition of the northern star in the southern sky; the successful planting of a new strain of avocado on the eastern hill slopes of Peru; the re-evaluation of the goal, purpose and direction of European literature; the birth of sextuplet boys in a small village in Venezuela, each boy having on his left buttock a perfect strawberry-coloured birthmark which, under a magnifying glass and in certain lights, appeared to represent the initial letters of the name of Jesus Christ Our Lord and Saviour, written in the Cyrillic alphabet; the impregnation of a twelve-year old virgin whose hymen, upon medical examination, was proven to be intact; the recovery of the Amazonian rain-forest and the subsequent successful re-establishment of the Andean Mahogany and Banana Exporting Company; the complete collapse of the international cocaine-smuggling industry; and, perhaps the most remarkable of all, the sudden and completely unpredictable reduction to zero of the illiteracy rate in each and every province of Colombia in which his words were reported.

Perhaps the real reason why Pigafetta did not describe this creature is that, amongst all the many and extraordinary creatures which he did describe, and in the describing of which his wonder and amazement is fully evident, this particular creature quite simply confounded him beyond plausibility, and stretched his gullibility too far (or was he simply overawed by the tales he heard, and recognised that this was not a mere creature at all, but a genuine manifestation of the demiurge?) This is not surprising. Even Borges, himself a South American and therefore natively accustomed to the sight of such fantastic creatures, found him too extraordinary to include in his Encyclopaedia Of Mythic And Imaginary Beings; an encyclopaedia which does include spherical-shaped beasts, griffons, and even a celestial stag, but makes no mention of this unnatural phenomenon.

Who, then - or rather what - is it - or he? Aesthetic evidence in the writings of Alejo Carpentier seems to point to the immediate literary origins of this creature; although certain passages of the Quixote, certain tales in

Boccaccio's "Decameron", and the poetry of the Chilean poet-statesman Pablo Neruda, likewise bear traces of the roots of this same genetic strain; though none quite so much so as the North American novelist William Faulkner.

But all this presumes the creature to be just an incidence of fiction, denying it an authentic flesh-and-blood existence. Certainly the remote Colombian village of Aracataca claims to be the creature's birthplace, but this must be discounted; the name is too lyrical, too musical, and far too aesthetically symmetrical, and must therefore be considered as an act of biographer's hyperbole rather than a genuine explication of the mystery. Yet certain details are known. Sightings of the creature at the National University in Bogota in the 1940s have now been confirmed (although rumours that the creature was capable of performing shamanistic and magic acts, of drinking up to a dozen bottles of tequila without becoming drunk, and that, during its time there, it fathered twenty-seven sons and eighteen daughters on forty-five different women, all of whom bore the name Ursula Remedios Buendia, are surely unfounded). The creature has been seen in places as far apart as Barcelona and Havana, is alleged to have participated in a certain television soap opera of dubious quality but considerable popularity, and once, while receiving the Nobel Prize for Literature at the Royal Palace in Stockholm, began its speech with a commentary on a book by one Antonio Pigafetta, a Florentine navigator who went with Magellan on the first voyage around the world, and who wrote, upon his passage through the southern lands of America, a strictly accurate account that nonetheless resembles a venture into fantasy.

Among the fifty-five wars, the two hundred and seventeen military coups, the deaths of twenty million children before the age of one, the six hundred and thirty thousand disappeared persons, the two and a half million refugees, the four million wet-backs, the eighty million slum-dwellers, the seventy-seven lost or decimated tribes, the millions of square kilometres of uninhabitable or infertile marsh, mountain, desert and rain-forest, the fourteen sacked cities, the three hundred excommunicated priests, the two hundred thousand forced migrants, the one and a quarter million political prisoners, and the dreams of several thousand would-be juntas, regimes and outright dictatorships to dominate alone the whole of El Dorado - among all this the creature doesn't seem so fantastical after all, but a mere man who, like his master Faulkner, "declines to accept the end of Man". The name of this creature is Marquez. In him resides the hope and future of South American - even, perhaps, world - literature.

THE TRIAL

A man - perhaps Thomas More or Tycho Brahé, perhaps Jesus Christ Himself or some priest of Marxist Theology in South America - is tried by a censorious and conservative government - perhaps the Inquisition, perhaps the Cromwellites, perhaps Fascists, perhaps Communists; it matters not a jot. They have put him on trial because they wish to stop the spread of an idea which they perceive as being harmful - though whether harmful to the general public, or merely harmful to the status quo that corroborates their authority, it isn't for us to say. The man goes heroically to the scaffold, refusing to recant his great idea; and his martyrdom - for what other name can we give it? - has the opposite effect to that intended: the idea spreads, albeit in misunderstood formulations and well-intentioned variations. Until, at last, the idea has gained universal acclaim, and the martyr has been deified.

And does it then matter that the day will come when the idea too is put on trial, and proven false?

THE MEETING

According to the "Norman Chronicle", an adjunct to the earlier and better known "Anglo-Saxon Chronicle", the two brothers Geoffroy and Halbert de Goncourt made this solemn vow upon their departure from Crecy: that each would raise an army, to overthrow the tyrant John and restore his elder brother Richard to his rightful throne; that they wouldn't meet again until - and the precise words they used, though intended romantically rather than literally, are especially significant - they came "face to face, on the steps of John's palace, a year to the day hence".

And so it fell out. Louis, King of France, offered Geoffroy his support, providing him with a thousand lancers, a thousand infantry, and a thousand cavalry, plus ships to carry them across the Channel into England. Philippe, Duke of Burgundy, precisely matched these numbers in favour of the younger brother Halbert, and in addition promised him his daughter Eleanor for a wife should he prove victorious.

The two brothers parted company on the first day of September. Their armies were raised and ready by March. Equinoctial tides prevented their setting sail across the Channel before April. Supporters of the tyrant John kept them embattled, the one in Cornwall, the other in Kent, until late summer. But on the last day of August, unbeknown to each other, the two brothers led their armies, from diametrically opposite directions, in final assault upon the king's stronghold at Winchester.

That afternoon, in separate battles, the two brothers were defeated. The King ordered that they be beheaded, and, the following day, the anniversary of their agreement, their severed heads were stuck up on poles, facing each other, at the foot of the steps of King John's palace.

THE MANUSCRIPT

His name was Reb David Tsvi Meir ben Yakov, and he was known as the Datsmay, from an acronym of his initials, and as the Maggid of Ayn Choshech, from his book about the Holocaust which had made his literary reputation.

When Reb David died he was told he could take only one of his manuscripts with him to Heaven. His songs and poems he left behind, because they were of small merit; his essays and commentaries and polemics he left behind, because they had been written for men and were best left in the hands of men; his novels too he left behind, because they were works of the imagination and he wouldn't take anything that wasn't absolutely veracious into the Palace of Truth. He chose to take the book he'd called "Ayn Choshech" (an untranslatable pun: literally "The Well of Darkness", or "The Eye of Darkness"; but, spoken, "Ayn" may also mean "there is no..."). Why this book? Because it was itself a Book of Judgement, and just as he had judged others in writing the book, so it was right and proper that he in turn should be judged by it. Yet he took it with reservations, because absolute veracity isn't given to Mankind.

Arriving at the gates of Heaven, he was met by the patriarch Moses, who asked to see the manuscript, and enquired what exactly it contained.

"It's an account of the Holocaust," Reb David explained, "through the life of a character I made up from an amalgamation of many real characters, a German Jew who fought against the Nazis and survived the extermination camps and made aliya to Israel and died there of his wounds."

At once Moses opened the gates of Heaven to welcome him inside.

"I too know what it is to be delivered out of bondage," Moses told him. "For writing this you are worthy of a place in Heaven. Pure fact or partial fiction, there were six million who really did die in that Holocaust, and we are all the inheritors of their memory, we all weep for their terrible fates. In writing this you have performed a mitzvah, for your account reveals the truth, and through it the memory of those days will be kept alive by the generations to come."

Gratified by these remarks, Reb David entered Heaven, and it wasn't long before he encountered the patriarch Abraham, who asked what was in the manuscript, and received the same reply that Moses had received.

"Sodom and Gomorrah!" Abraham cried, pronouncing those two names as though they caused him pain. "You shouldn't have written such a book," he went on. "Couldn't you have found even five good Germans, and told their stories? The dead are dead, but Germany lives on, Germany must have the means to find redemption for its heinous sin. Five righteous gentiles. Couldn't you have chosen to honour even one of these by telling his or her true story? Had you done so, then you would have performed a deed worthy of salvation and a place in Heaven."

Reb David continued on his way towards the palace of the Almighty, and soon enough he came upon the patriarch Isaac.

"What's that manuscript you're carrying?" Isaac asked him.

And Red David told him what he'd already told Moses and Abraham.

"Ah, yes," Isaac responded sadly. "I know what it is to have been such a man. I too was taken to such a trial. I too was fortunate enough to survive. One never really recovers, you know, from such an experience. But my story was my story, not someone else's. How dare you write about this when you've never experienced it? How dare you presume to imagine what such a trial must have been like? Better that you'd been there yourself, better that you'd survived to tell your own story. Then I would have judged in your favour and not simply welcomed you into Heaven. Then you would have merited a place among the saints."

At last Reb David reached the Palace of Justice and the throne of the Almighty, but there he found only darkness and silence, no angels, none of the joy he had anticipated. No, there was only the Almighty, crouched on the floor in the darkest corner of the palace, dressed in sackcloth and with His garments rent, a heap of dust and ashes enshrouding Him so deep that He could scarcely breathe. In His hand He held a pen, and on His lap there lay an open book which Reb David could see at once was the Book of Life, a new book as it seemed, in which not a single letter had yet been written. Reb David waited for the Almighty to speak or summon him, but there came neither sign nor whisper for what seemed like an eternity. But then, at last, the Almighty turned His head and slowly, painfully, raised His arm to receive the manuscript, and glanced through it, and sighed.

"So it was this one that you chose," He said. "I knew it would be. I knew you would leave all the love poems and the beautiful lyrics and the descriptions of nature behind, and bring only this work to judgement. How many of you must there be who come like this, like Job, to torment me, bearing your novels and your essays and your lists of dates and numbers and your endless, endless poems of protest! But you, you are the worst, you are the cruellest of all my torturers. The others at least wrote the truth, stories of real people who actually lived and died, whose blood is on my hands, whose cries are in my heart. But you, you have to be different, you have to do better than that! Why did you have to write this - a fiction, an invented character? Do I not already have six million on my conscience? Did you really have to add one more name to the numbers of the dead?"

Then Reb David took a burning coal from among the cinders on the floor, and he set fire to the pages of his manuscript, one by one. And lo, out of the darkness of the palace of almighty justice, there flickered the tiniest glow of light.

THE LABYRINTH

The legend of Theseus and the Minotaur is no longer so well-known that one may speak of it without first reiterating it.

King Minos of Crete hated the people of Athens, for they had killed his son when he won all the prizes at the Athenian games. To prevent him from making war against them, the Athenians sent seven youths and seven maidens each year to be sacrificed to the Minotaur - a creature who was half man and half bull - which inhabited King Minos' labyrinth on the island of Crete. Theseus, son of King Aegeus of Athens, swore to kill the Minotaur and thereby end this tyranny. Storms wracked his ship, but failed to wreck it. Upon landing at Crete he met the King's daughter, Ariadne, and the two promptly fell in love; Ariadne swore to help Theseus against the Minotaur, and gave him a sword, a ball of magic thread, and a promise of marriage should he return. Like Hansel and Gretel in the wood, Theseus used the magic thread as a road-marker for the labyrinth. He found the Minotaur at last, struggled with it long and fiercely, and did eventually prevail. Following the trail of his magic thread he emerged victorious from the labyrinth and claimed his bride.

This is the tale, and from it Theseus has come down to us in myth as the master of the labyrinth. Now, another myth, recently discovered on four parchments from the excavations at Knossos, would appear to corroborate, even to accentuate this reputation. According to this myth, at the time of the Spartan siege of Athens, when all seemed lost, Theseus, now King of Athens, challenged Archimetorus, King of Sparta, to a trial of strength upon which the fate and freedom of their city-states would depend, winner-take-all. The parchments tell very little, and all are damaged or incomplete, but enough is readable for us to know that Theseus subjected Archimetorus to a gladiatorial joust against himself and six of his fiercest warriors; Archimetorus killed the six, and held his knife to Theseus' throat.

"They say you're the master of the labyrinth," Archimetorus mocked. "So I shall not kill you. I have designed a labyrinth for you, complete with monsters. You may take your sword. You may take your magic thread. For all I care you may take Ariadne your wife as well. I assure you, you will not find a way out, for it is without doubt an inescapable maze."

Archimetorus laughed, and ordered Theseus to be bound, along with Ariadne. They were taken aboard a ship, sailed towards the Orient, then led on foot into the very heart of the Arabian desert. Their captors abandoned them there without food or water, nor the means of making a shelter. Sandstorms swept the desert for thousands of square miles, washing away the footprints of their departed captors.

How did the story end? The parchments do not tell us. All that is known is that Sparta held Athens in thrall for seven years, seven months and seven days, at the end of which time a man claiming to be an emissary of King Theseus arrived at the palace of King Archimetorus, bearing four gifts. The first was a spool of magic thread. The second was a woman in Arab dress, who upon removal of her veil proved to be Ariadne. The third was the revelation of the emissary as Theseus himself. The fourth was his sword.

BEYOND THE THRESHOLD

You approach the house cautiously in the darkness, levering a half-open window wide enough to squeeze your body through. You pick up small items of jewellery, precious ornaments, electrical goods, and for half an hour or more you transport them in complete silence to the vehicle outside. From one upstairs room you hear the sound of snoring, and turn away. In two others you continue making your illicit acquisitions. You enter the last room, believing it to be empty, but it turns out to be occupied by a young woman, sleeping soundly, lying on her side. You are entranced by her good looks and excellent figure and now, newly emboldened by an hour's free roaming in the house, the sight of her excites you to still more daring deeds. You lift the blankets from the girl, who stirs slightly but does not wake. You accost her, holding your hand firmly over her mouth and your knife to her throat when, inevitably, your interference wakens her. Done, you slit her throat, taking care not to let any blood splash on your clothing. Then a moment's panic seizes you that forensic clues must lie about, and for your own protection you return to the vehicle, recover a five gallon can of petrol, and sprinkle the girl's body, the carpets, the gas taps, the path to the front gate. From the vehicle's window you throw a flaming box of matches at the petrol trail, and drive away with all speed. Only someone on the corner has seen you. Mysteriously a gun appears in your hand and you shoot the watcher through the head. But the sound of gunfire is so like the sound of your neighbour's car, its exhaust backfiring as it does every weekday dawn, that the similarity begins to alter your state of consciousness. Already the burning house has gone. The slaughtered family have gone too. Even the stolen goods in the back of the vehicle have gone, along with that momentary quiver of surprise at yourself for having perpetrated all these deeds. Gradually you come fully awake, and your memory retains no trace whatsoever of the dream. It never happened. Were you to read these lines, they would strike no chord, incite not even the vaguest recognition. Cold and still tired you rise, dress, wash, eat breakfast, and resume the normalities of your utterly respectable life.

A DON JUAN OF THE IMAGINATION

He was a man of enormous culture and sophistication. You could tell that he was also profound by the remarkable paucity of cultural ornaments with which he surrounded himself - "more than plenty for one lifetime", as he was wont to say. The room where he "hung his painting" (his preferred phrase, uttered invariably with an ironic laugh), consisted only of a reproduction of an early Jackson Pollock - the art school of which he was a patron held a scholarship exam each year, the winning of which depended on a candidate's ability to make a perfect facsimile of the Pollock, not by copying the painting but by replicating the arbitrary and random methodology of its creation. His collection of music extended no further than a set of Bach fugues, the Wagner Ring-Cycle (which he refused to play), and Mahler's 2nd Symphony - "the three works that contain all the possibilities of music, all the moods, all the variations, all the history of music, and are therefore quite sufficient for a lifetime." And in his library just three books, Melville's "Moby-Dick", an edition of the "Bhagavad Gita", and - and here I must express amazement as well as pride - my own "Argaman Quintet".

I met him only the once - the day I delivered him my book at his request. We talked, over sips of porter wine, of love and literature.

"The key," he told me, "isn't to read, but to re-read. No book, no work of art, no suite of music, is ever the same twice. The fact that we've encountered it before changes our apprehension of it on the next occasion. And besides, encountering it makes us different, alters our inner state, and so it's never the same person who is making the encounter."

He taught poetry by making his protégés copy out verse verbatim, the way they make painters learn at art schools. Likewise he insisted that no one should ever attempt to read a novel with the eyes alone, but always to approach it with a pen in hand. Before I left he showed me his manuscript of the Gita, written out both in English italics and a copperplate Sanskrit (he didn't understand the Sanskrit as language), and the four different copies of the Melville that had taken him all of sixty years (I was surprised how poor his handwriting had been when he was young).

For so eclectic a man, for a man with such a reputation as an aesthete, these precise limits that he placed upon his erudition may well seem surprising. Yet surely, as he would himself have said, it was precisely these limits that so liberated him, that gave him such breadth. Nor, in the light of the above, should it astonish the reader to learn that this notoriously passionate worshipper of women had married at the age of seventeen, and remained entirely faithful to his "beloved Sophia" until they died, within weeks of each other, both well into their nineties.

I write this obituary in his honour, and through him hope to honour all who share his catholic tastes.

NOSTRADAMUS

It is one of the peculiarities of human physiology that a man may be morally or physically blind and intellectually long-sighted at one and the same time. Such is the well-documented case of Tiresias, the seer of Thebes. Such too is the case of the 17th century French seer Michel de Nostradame, known to the world as Nostradamus; though in this instance he wasn't blind, but merely myopic.

Looking into the darkness of his crystal ball, Nostradamus saw with total clarity the entire future of human history, and at the same time understood with perfect insight the dangerous impact of announcing it; for if to wish that something might happen is to reduce the likelihood of its happening, then it follows logically that to openly predict it is to ensure that it does not, indeed that it cannot happen. And more importantly, to leave out of his predictions certain events which he had also seen, was to ensure that they could still happen. And here he faced an immense moral dilemma, for Nostradamus' aim was only to read the future, not to interfere with it.

So he saw Napoleon and deliberately misread it as Napolloron, saw Hitler and misread Hister. So, with alarming frequency, he made his references oblique and even obscure – "the wall that divides a city" for example, could as easily be Jerusalem as Berlin, or metaphorically that of Belfast or Sarajevo. Some critics allege that this obfuscation was a symptom of moral weakness; others, less mincing with their words, have accused him outright of failing to prevent some of the grossest calumnies of human history, and as such of bearing personal responsibility for them. But this is unfair. Even if the man was morally short-sighted, still he read as best he could in the darkness of his own room and the darkness of the future and the darkness of the human soul. And besides, even a prophet may not claim unto himself the right to interfere in human history. His task is to forewarn, not to forestall. And can we not logically presume that, if the future is foreseeable, then it must be predetermined; and that if it is predetermined, then the preordained scheme must surely include both Nostradamus and the particular way he chose to disclose it?

But there is also much for us to be grateful for. Nostradamus foresaw the outbreak of the Third World War, foresaw each one of the key stages that would lead up to that catastrophe, foresaw too the complete destruction of the planet that would ensue: and predicted every detail explicitly to ensure that it would not happen. He also, to take but two contemporary events, saw but did not describe the demise of the seventy-four year experiment in Russian Communism, nor the impending reunification of Charlemagne's European Empire under German hegemony. Nor, it is interesting to note, did he comment at any time on

Jewish history, which is strange, for he was himself a Jew and must surely have wished to intercede. Or perhaps it was simply that he took some things for granted: the centuries of eternal wandering, the millennia of perpetual persecution, the yellow star, the ghettos. Perhaps even he could not believe, on looking into the glass, that there could be a Jewish homeland in the State of Israel. Or perhaps he did believe, and chose to remain silent, lest one man - himself - should be responsible for preventing what only the coming of the Messiah Himself could bring to pass.

THE TURIN SHROUD

During the summer and autumn of 1988, scientists examined the famous Turin Shroud - and proved that it was a fake. The shroud was thought to have been that of Jesus, the image on it that of the Saviour himself, miraculously transferred to the shroud by the mere fact of a god being wrapped in it. By process of carbon dating, however, it was demonstrated that the cloth of the shroud was manufactured no earlier than the thirteenth, and perhaps as late as the fourteenth century post domini, though by whom has not yet been established (the contention that it was Leonardo Da Vinci may be attributed to the simple-mindedness of modern man who, believing that the pre-Renaissance was an age of general intellectual darkness, cannot imagine more than one human genius who might have enlightened it).

However, such rationalist-empiricist theorising cannot explain the mystery, even though it may believe that it has explained the mystery away; for we are dealing here not with science but with the miracle of an image that can resurrect itself, transform itself, even change its appearance. In attempting to prove a mere forgery, scientific research into the shroud has in fact achieved the opposite. For science is limited by the simplicitudes of human knowledge and imagination, whereas God is entirely omniscient and omnipotent. For it wasn't intended that the body of Jesus should leave its shadow on the shroud, but a chance flash of lightning caused the miracle, and a mere divine tampering with carbon decomposition allowed God to delude Man into attributing the shroud's manufacture to Leonardo.

THE QUARE

In Celtic folklore, the name Connolly denotes descent from the grey seal. In Scottish tradition a quare is a gathering of poets for the purpose of reciting their epics and ballads, sometimes accompanied, sometimes unaccompanied, and of celebrating the greatness of all forms of Scottish culture in the appropriate manner. I explain these two facts only that my tale be more easily comprehensible - if, indeed, comprehensibility were an intended goal.

At Hogmanay in the year 876, five of the great Caledonian clans agreed to hold a quare the following midsummer's eve, and to gather in from all parts of the Celtic world the greatest scribes and poets who bore their families' names: mac Alpin, Aedan, Connolly, Dalriada. They came, they sang, they drank, they revelled. On the third day the Gaelic poet John Connolly arrived, apologetically late and apparently unseen in his arrival. He was toasted, made welcome, invited to contribute his portion to the quare.

The song that Connolly sang that night has never been written down, nor has oral tradition, so diligent in rescuing so much Celtic poetry from oblivion, recalled it. All that is known is the legend of the poem, and of the poet. Connolly's poem was entitled "The Seal". He spoke of the seal's capacity to dive to great depths and then to return, so very slowly, to the surface, bringing with him whatever it is he has discovered; he spoke of the several layers of fat which every seal so carefully grows, to protect himself where he feels most vulnerable; he spoke of the seal's extraordinary sense of touch, and the long, strong down of hair around the seal's mouth, highly sensitive even to the most gentle contact...and as he spoke a dim awareness came over his audience that this wasn't a man describing a mammal of the seas, but rather doing what all great poetry should do, which is to look inwards through the mirror of language and describe the soul and mind and body of the poet himself. It was, without doubt, one of the supreme moments of poetry, and his listeners were enraptured. Even the description of the seal's long whiskers, his translucent flesh, his changes of colour from pup to bull, seemed less a description of the creature than the man.

And when he had finished speaking, it is said, John Connolly threw off his clothes, revealing the perfect body of a grey Atlantic seal, and dived into the waters of the Irish sea, never to be heard or seen again.

THE CAPTIVE BRIDE

No sooner was she born than he seized her and stole her away. He tied her with an immense coil of thread, elastic enough that it could stretch as she grew, growing with her like a second skin. For years he kept her imprisoned in the darkness and fetor of his tiny home, feeding her only as little as was needed to sustain life and limb, waiting. Then, as soon as she reached puberty, he satisfied himself upon her, again and again for many days, until he was certain that he had impregnated her. So he abandoned her. But by now the elastic cords had stretched almost to their limits, and as her pregnancy enlarged her, so the cords broke. Alone, lying in her own filth, but at last free, she gave birth. How soon, she wondered, how soon would it be before he returned, or there came another like him, to snatch away her child and...

Were this a merely human tale, you, my reader, would no doubt censure me - if not actually censor me - for glorifying uxoriphobia, or at least for promulgating misogyny. However this is not a human tale. What are recorded above are the factual details of the normal sex life of the spider.

OLD MARTIN

Old Martin had a grand-daughter who was seventeen when she ran away from home. The girl's mother, who was Old Martin's daughter, was distraught. But Old Martin told her not to worry, as he would easily find the girl.

"What was she wearing when she left? What colour shoes? Was she carrying a bag? Did she make any telephone calls this morning?" Old Martin asked her, and a dozen more such questions besides. The mother answered all of them, until Old Martin felt that there was not a detail of the girl's life on the day of her departure that he didn't know - except, of course, her whereabouts. But even they were already obvious, for she had left behind an immense trail of signposts and scent-marks that even the least able of tracker dogs would have been able to follow.

Old Martin set out on foot, turning left or right as his intuition guided him. He spoke to many people on the way, adding further detail to the detail he'd brought with him. On the third evening he knocked at the door of a house, and asked for his grand-daughter by name.

"I've come to take you home," Old Martin told her.

"How did you find me?" the girl asked, amazed.

"I followed your tracks."

"But I left no tracks, grandpa," the girl replied. "I ran away from home. I walked for hours. When I got tired I took the first bus that came along and got off wherever it happened to stop. I allowed the first kind person who offered me help to take me home. I don't myself know where I am exactly. I left no tracks."

Old Martin smiled and, taking her by the hand, began to lead her home.

This incident took place, not along the songlines of aboriginal Australia, but between Hackney and Clapham, in London, in 1993.

THE INDEX

The Argaman Press proudly presents its unique catalogue of writings which, according to the highest authorities of their days, constitute some of the greatest masterpieces of all time, the equals of Shakespeare, Dante, Molière...

"La Grande Bataille de Crecy"; author or authors unknown, probably written down in the late 13th century but originating much earlier, it is held to be the greatest of all works in the troubadour style of poetry, though unusual in that it departs from the customary themes of love and romance to speak of the massacre of the Celtic French (Armoricans) by the Angevins (Normans).

"The Gospel According to St James"; written in Greek and originally published in Egypt, James' account of the life of his master is characteristically different from the better known synoptic gospels, particularly in its insistence on what may be termed gnostic conceptions. The book first appeared in Europe in about 1400 CE; many scholars hold it to be a fake.

"La Saga di Gabrielle" by Roberto di Guislano; a 14th century Italian romance which sought to merge the Commedia Dell'Arte and Condottiere traditions of Italian theatre and prose. It tells the story of the archangel Gabriel, sent by God to announce the birth of Jesus to Mary, and of how he fell deeply, and carnally, in love with her, ultimately fathering the child himself.

"Tempus Fugit" by Guiseppe di Scarlatto; an early 15th century Italian tractate which promulgated the notion, gleaned as so much Renaissance culture was from the Arabic, that time is less important than action, and that the person who carries out the action is the least important of all.

"The Virgin Mary Magdalene", a poem by the 15th century Flemish poet Richard Van Der Elk, in which it is imagined that the two Marys of Christian tradition were in fact one and the same.

"Antonio" by Mordechai Levy; written in 1634 but never performed in England, it presented a riposte to Shakespeare's story of "The Merchant of Venice" from a Jewish perspective.

"Against Slavery: A Polemic" by Brahame Swift. Unlike his elder brother, Jonathan, Brahame wrote but one book. A marginal note in the journals of William Wilberforce suggests that copies of the book were circulated privately over several decades. Wilberforce himself was powerfully influenced by its coherent and lyrical attack on all forms of human slavery, including, interestingly, marriage.

"Gott Ohne Ich, Ich Ohne Gott" by Hermann Dietrich Fassbinder. A 19th century German essay in novel form which arguably was the first modern work to establish atheism as a defensible intellectual posture.

"The Princess Clementine Rose"; an otherwise run-of-the-mill romance by one of the 19th century's lesser known women novelists, Mary Graveney; it enjoyed a brief *succes de scandale* for its unusually graphic descriptions of lesbian love.

"The Complete Poems of Osip Mandelstam." Only about a tenth of Mandelstam's oeuvre has survived his persecution at the hands of Stalin. This volume brings the remainder together for the first time.

All of these works - and many, many more - are offered by us as titles only, as the manuscripts are alas no more. What all these works have in common is their unavailability, and the reason for their unavailability. They share a common fate. What might otherwise have been handed down to us as some of the greatest masterworks of European culture may now only be savoured, relished, deified, as titles. Each of these works was banned, burned or prescribed by the particular authorities of their day, because they were perceived as challenging those authorities, or the status quo, or as being inflammatory and therefore dangerous to the common reader. What remains is an index, utterly mouth-watering, though alas not mouth-watering enough to quench the fires in which they burned.

THE INEXPLICABLE

On the shoreline floats the body of the Great Pharaoh Rameses II, King of Egypt, builder of the "great pyramid", rationalist and empiricist, master of geometry and logic, man of science and the material world. The greatest mind of the ancient world has been destroyed by mystery, slain by the impossible, drowned in a flood that could not have taken place. This man who denied the inexplicable has been inexplicably defeated by it.

Rameses does not believe in magic; if he keeps magicians at his court, it's only to frighten foreigners and to amuse his many wives. Rameses does not believe in gods, though he knows how superstitious all his various peoples are, and so he tolerates their worship of all manner of absurd divinities; for himself he worships only Akhenaton, the disc of the sun, the pulse that beats in all living things, and which gives and takes away life. Yet even Akhenaton he doesn't conceive of as a god, but merely as a metaphor. Rameses does not hold with religion. All things have a rational explanation. Man is God. And especially the man Rameses.

When the stammerer out-wizarded his wizards, devoured their snakes with his snakes, out-prophesied their prophecies with his prophecies, Rameses laughed because wizards and magic snakes and prophecies were only children's tricks. He did not believe in them as reality, and so he did not let the stammerer's people go. When the water turned to blood, he knew it was no god but the result of some tribal massacre in the far mountains. When the frogs and lice and wild beasts and pestilence and boils and hail and locusts came, one after the next, to plague his people, he understood that these were the normal trials inflicted by nature upon itself, and he ordered his doctors to prepare more and better medicines. When the land was plunged in total darkness, Rameses watched in fascination from his palace roof for the slow passing of the eclipse. When his first-born son died in an epidemic that broke out one dark night, and vanished as quickly in the morning, he comforted himself with the knowledge that the first-born sons of Egypt were made for sacrificing anyway, and the boy, already twelve, had barely months to live. When the slaves mutinied, led by what all the tablets were convinced was his own illegitimate grandson, he accepted that this was the inevitable consequence of his persistent refusal to set them free, and knew that they couldn't flee further than the Red Sea, where he would easily recapture them.

Everything is explicable. Everything, perhaps, but not this: why, after witnessing so many sham mysteries, so many fraudulently miraculous events, so many apparently paranormal phenomena, and being able to dismiss each one of them with a perfectly rational explanation; why did the great Pharaoh Rameses, King of Egypt, builder of the "great pyramid", rationalist and empiricist, master of geometry and logic, man of science and the material world, why did he come up to the shores of the Red Sea, and perceive the optical illusion that the waters had somehow parted to make a path, and still give the order to his men to cross?

THE UNICORN

From the travel journals of R.P. Narayan (Tibet 1874)

We came at last upon a land beyond those mountains, a land so far cut off from humankind it can only have been by chance we did not miss it. The land was poorer than any we had yet encountered, the earth a fine sand in which it hardly seemed that anything could grow. Half-naked men toiled in the fields, themselves strapped to the ploughs in teams of four, dragging the heavy chains across their shoulders while the women, embalmed while still alive in layers of tribal clothing, marched along in front upon their knees, removing stones too large and jagged for the plough to cut through.

Then it was we found the proof of which we'd come in search, a single-antlered deer of immense beauty, standing idly under a tree and chewing grass as though for all the world this land were Paradise and grass a substance very much in surfeit.

"The unicorn!" I cried out, and might have rushed to put my arms around the beast and hug it, only one of the natives heard my cry, and in response to it he turned and fixed his gaze in what could only be interpreted as fury on the beast. His look brought me up with a start, and I stood still in horror as I watched him take his rifle from his shoulder, and shoot the creature dead.

"You've shot the unicorn!" I exclaimed, something in the tone of voice his fellow sailors must have used towards the Ancient Mariner.

The man spat on the ground, and I was stammering incoherently:

"Shot the unicorn. How can? Unique? We travel years. Whole world in search. The unicorn. The unicorn."

He was looking at me as though I'd gone mad. Later another of the natives explained to me that the unicorn was pandemic in the land; they bred without cease, usually twins or triplets; they lived to a phenomenal old age; the natives had tried to drive them over the mountain, but they seemed only to want to live in this one place. The unicorn was responsible for the state of the land, for the condition of servitude to nature in which all men and women lived and died. It had become an unspoken law amongst these people that to see a unicorn was already to have shot it, and in the winter whole armies of hunters went into the forests to undertake organised massacres of these rodent beasts.

THE RABBI

The Rabbi prayed alone, for prayer, he liked to say, is a dialogue between Man and God, and other people shouldn't eavesdrop upon personal and private conversations.

Now the law of minyan, or quorum, states quite clearly that a man should never pray alone, but only when a minimum of ten are gathered together. So the Rabbi recited Elohey Avoteynu, and Abraham, Isaac and Jacob appeared. He uttered the Shema, and behold Moses. He recited a Psalm, and silent trumpets ushered in King David. He sang Yigdal, and the Rambam joined the congregation. He said Kaddish, and his father entered. He davened the Amidah, and the Messiah appeared. And himself, of course. And opening the Ark made ten.

The Rabbi prayed, and he was not alone, for he had invoked the souls of the holiest and the most righteous, who stood beside him now in solemn assembly. He prayed, confessing and attesting in the name of his community, offering himself as watchman of the city, spokesman for his tribe, scapegoat for his people, heir of the lost generations and father of the generations still to come.

The Rabbi prayed alone, and the whole world was admitted to his solitary dialogue.

A NEW VERSION OF SISYPHUS

For the umpteenth time Sisyphus pondered the approaching summit. Each journey had followed a slightly different course whilst remaining essentially the same journey - now through the gorse and bracken, now through the pine spinneys, now between the rocks where his own rock became the rock of ages; now singing and collecting snow-flowers and purple amethyst, now puffing and panting in a desolation more sheer even than the jagged cliffs. This journey had gone more slowly than some, bogged down by rain and distracted for long stretches by the long stretches of the long legs of that most beautiful shepherdess he had come to know better with each journey, she eternally taking her sheep down the mountain where he rolled his rock eternally upwards. So the summit approached; the sadness of a pleasant journey's ending; the preparation of his mind to re-descend and make another journey up as sweet as possible; the keen anticipation of the shepherdess' promised favours counter-balanced by the relentless backward-rolling of the rock, heavier than any crucifix. So he was surprised to see the winged messenger awaiting him on the summit. So he was shocked to hear that Athens had fallen, the gods had been expelled, Olympus conquered, all edicts overturned, including the one that set the terms of his own punishment. Eternity, apparently, had ended. He was set free.

Yet what more could he have wanted than such mountain sweetness, a girl, a goal? Once more he cursed the gods who had forsaken him, and pressed on.

THE BOOK OF DAYS

Rummaging through the shelves in the *Libraria Judaica*, I came upon a Book of Days - less an almanac than a commemorative calendar, recording for each day of the year an historical event. It threw up some fascinating data - of the sort from which Calvino might have made an essay. Two days ago, for example, on January 13th, Emile Zola published "J'accuse" in defence of Dreyfus; a letter clearly in vain, since yesterday the Church of Rome confiscated and burned all Jewish books (I would quote, in reference to this, Heine's famous prediction that "where they begin by burning books, they will end by burning people"; however it's only January 15th, and he hasn't said it yet.)

Predicting the future is a fatuous superstition, albeit one that produces much childish amusement. The past, on the other hand, is much safer territory, especially when it's contiguous with the present. Thus it's extraordinary to learn that Friday the 19th will see the first resistance in the Warsaw Ghetto, an event that will lead, in less than seven days, to the liberation of Auschwitz by the Russians.

There is much scope here for an interesting retelling of history. A year book gives each day a commemorative significance that is repeated year after year immutably, so that it's as if there's only that year, and events precede and succeed each other with a timelessness not apparent in chronological history. Thus, Henry II forbade Jews in England to build synagogues, just four days before Cromwell confirmed their right of residence. Thus Einstein was born the day before Scharansky was arrested. Thus eighty Jews were massacred at Bray on the very day following Napoleon's decree allowing them French citizenship. It's simply a matter of years losing their flux and being replaced by constancy - a notion useless equally to physicists and metaphysicians, but tremendously exciting to mere authors.

Tomorrow, I note, they will open a new synagogue in Madrid, the first since Columbus set sail for foreign shores; it seems oddly heroic in its futility however, since the date of the final exile from Spain has already been set for August 2nd.

ROBIN HOOD

The idea of the criminal who is essentially good, but who nevertheless commits evil, is an integral part of the English tradition, perhaps because the natural sanguine of the Anglo-Saxon, coupled with his Protestant faith in Mankind's ultimate goodness, inclines him towards the humanistic. Despite, or - given that this is sanguine we are speaking of - perhaps because of the histories of Crippen, Christie, Sweeney Todd and all the other psychopathic cut-throats whose heads have, so to speak, graced the ornamental block on Tower Hill, there remains a deep nostalgia for the memory of Robin Hood, the criminal who acts out of high moral dudgeon, and a great respect for those who, like McVicar, return penitently to the fold after completing their requisite periods of imprisonment.

At his trial in May 1934, acting in his own defence, Peter Willard made a summing-up speech that lasted more than forty minutes, and which was later described by Judge Malcolm Wainwright as being "as brilliant in its lucidity as it was cunning in its conception", in which he sought to justify his criminal misdeeds as "an act of rebellion against a world that reveres love without first trying to understand hatred". Reluctantly, and only after both the police before the trial and the prosecution lawyers during it had exerted considerable pressure, he acknowledged that he was opposed to the government's economic strategy; that he believed the Wall St Crash and the ensuing Depression to have been examples of sublime if not divine justice; that he perceived the League of Nations as an international conspiracy by nationalists against those who favoured a global community; complained that he had been unable to find any employment commensurate with his abilities; and avowed repeatedly that he did not believe he had harmed anyone who was not morally impeachable to a greater degree than the punishment he had inflicted. Three times he made reference to the Jarrow March, twice to the Paris Commune of 1870, at least once to the Socialist Revolution, and quoted frequently from both Marx and St Augustine on the subjects of morality and metaphysics.

It was not, however, a political speech, for he was not a man inhibited by ideologies. His crimes, he maintained, struck a hammer-blow for those who had been humiliated with charity and compassion, those who had been deprived of solitude through an excess of unsolicited love or friendship, those who had been denied privacy by fame, those who had been exiled from real life and real feeling by exorbitant wealth, and all those others whose spiritual growth had been restricted by the indignity of happiness.

Two psychologists testified to his sanity; five reputable professional men gave excellent character references; the senior policeman investigating the case admitted that the crimes had been so brilliantly executed it would have been impossible to track down their perpetrator, if their perpetrator hadn't voluntarily surrendered himself; and even the counsel for the prosecution found himself complimenting Willard both for his prose style and, as he expressed it, "his admirable idealism and personal integrity". Nonetheless, facts were facts: he had broken into the home of the alleged international arms smuggler Justin Delange, removed more than half a million pounds in cash from his wall-safe, and left it on the steps of a local children's charity. He had set fire to seven brothels, three illegal gambling houses and four opium dens in the London area. He had cut the throats of no less than eleven gang-leaders from Merseyside to the Firth of Forth. He had...

After a trial lasting three months, and in which Peter Willard pleaded not guilty despite initially giving himself up to the police and making a full and detailed confession, it took the jury only seconds to agree by a nod of the head that he was guilty on all counts, and that there could be no mitigating circumstances nor acceptable pleas of diminished responsibility - as Willard fully agreed. His voluntary surrender was taken into account, as was the vital information given by him to the police which enabled them to complete all of their enquiries satisfactorily - he was sentenced to nine hundred and ninety nine years for murder, with a second sentence of fifteen years for arson, and a third of eight years for armed robbery, all of these to run concurrently. In the end he spent eighteen years as a guest of the Governor of Broadmoor, where he was held to be a model prisoner, twice recommended for parole by Members of Parliament, and three times champion of the prison chess tournament. He died of natural causes while still in custody, in June 1952.

THE UNIVERSAL PRINCIPLE

It is a truism so obvious that it hardly needs stating, that Mankind has been divided for as long as Mankind has existed, by wars of ideology: political, philosophical or religious. Men, and even sometimes women, fight to the very death (though rarely their own deaths; they forcibly conscript soldiers or hire mercenaries to die as their surrogates), to defend their cherished principles against those of the unprincipled enemy.

To give one obvious example: the Cold War, fought out in the fields of First World Propaganda and Third World Famine for more than half a century. The principles upon which the Soviet Union fought its corner, inspired by the writings of Marx and Lenin (writings which were themselves inspired by the philosophers of the European Enlightenment), were laid down in the Soviet Constitution of 1917; those of the United States of America, the principal as well as the principle adversary, inspired directly by the writings of the philosophers of the European Enlightenment, were enshrined in the American Constitution of 1776.

In 1948, all members of the United Nations Organisation - a body comprising Communists as well as Democrats, Christians as well as Moslems, Hindus, Atheists and even, when not boycotted, Jews - found themselves able to agree, and formally signed as a condition of their admission to the organisation and their ratification of its Charter, a Declaration of Human Rights, universally applicable, which likewise had its origins in the European Enlightenment. Thirty years later it was given solemn guarantee and further elaboration in the Helsinki Final Act.

By agreeing to this Universal Principle, each member state of the UNO endorsed what may be described as the Idealisation of a single view of Man and of Society; and through it a Divine, or Cosmic Harmony. For the Soviet Union this Principle was termed Socialist, as for the Vatican it manifested perfectly the essence of Christ's teachings, for the White House it defined Democracy, for Erasmus Humanism and for Sartre's followers Existentialism. The Aboriginals of Papua New Guinea had no more difficulty in accepting it as an elucidation of their own Way, than did Buddhists, Jains, worshippers of Shinto or Zoroaster or Tixo; while Moses and Plato, *inter alia*, had argued consistently for precisely such a statement, and both Diderot and Voltaire had long advocated it.

Though the name of the Ideology endorsing the Principle is different in each case, the overriding and underlying Principle remains the same, and in this Principle every people on Earth has expressed with one voice the kind of world it hopes to realise. What is different is never the goal, but only the perceived best means of achieving that goal, and the language in which it should be described. Yet the goal remains identical.

Now that the Universal Principle has been defined and authorised, may we look forward at last to the advent of the Messianic Age and the epoch of Universal Peace and Brotherhood?

THE EIGHTH DAY

"Today is the eighth day, but where is God?"

"God is resting."

"But God rested yesterday."

"And He's resting again today. And tomorrow. And the day after to-morrow. And for all days to come. For God's task was the Creation of the Universe, and on the sixth day it was done."

"Yes, it was done. But He can't simply rest. He remains responsible for what He has created."

"No. He has completed Creation, and He is Creation, and that is the end of God. But as the very final act of Creation He said: 'Let us make Man in our own image and likeness, and let Man bear responsibility for the fish of the sea and the birds of the air and the animals that walk the Earth, and every living thing.'"

Today is the eighth day of Creation, and Man is wondering why God still sits at rest.

Today is the eighth day of Creation, and God is wondering why Man still sits at rest.

Today is the eighth day of God.

Today is the first day of Man.

THE ROOM OF THE 1001 CLOCKS

The name was prolix and exaggerated. To achieve what he was seeking to achieve, the Emperor required neither the pointless literary allusion nor, indeed, that number of clocks. Seven hundred and twenty, in fact, were quite sufficient.

The room was circular. Its floor was of white marble, the colour of light. Its walls, save only for the occasional wooden frame without which they would not have remained upright, were made entirely of glass; the wooden frames were likewise painted the white of the marble. At the dead centre of the room, on a rectangular table, stood a sun-dial, though this, with its surrounding pool, was probably an ornamental joke - not a terribly good joke either, though considerably funnier than the herring, painted red, easily mistaken for koy carp, which inhabited the pool.

During the course of his reign, the Emperor had succeeded in fulfilling all the prophecies that had been handed down from generation to generation of emperors. He had subdued the barbarians to the north-east. He had crossed the western desert and built a second capital at the place where the date-palms ended and the sands began. He had conquered the mountain regions in order to eradicate the religious heresies incumbent there. He had established trade routes with the lands to the extreme west. He had located the princess of the golden slipper, and married her, and mourned her agonising death in childbirth.

All prophecies but one. For it was written that the emperor who achieved these things would not be condemned, as mortal men are otherwise condemned, to trudge from obscurity to oblivion. Rather he would live for ever, immortal and eternal as the gods. So the Emperor had fulfilled all the prophecies. So the Emperor had looked up in alarm when the imperial physician - he had executed one hundred and seventeen imperial physicians already, but now understood that they spoke not conspiracy but truth - informed him that the tumour in his stomach was malign, and gave him only months to live.

The purpose of the room - the ideogram is ambivalent and may be read as "sarcophagus" - was a last, heroic effort to fulfil the final prophecy, and to disprove the prognosis of the quacks. In addition to the sun-dial, the candle-clocks and the water-clocks - over none of which could the Emperor exercise control - seven hundred and twenty mechanical clocks had been procured, and each one allowed to stop, or else deliberately halted. Each face told its own moment, precisely one minute apart. In the room of the clocks, time had completely stopped even though time continued to move on. Whatever time it was, one of the clocks was always correct. Thus eternity was perfectly contained, and the body of the emperor, embalmed in its coffin, not dead but sleeping, on the table in the centre by the sun-dial.

THE KILLER

Among the literary papers of the great French auteur Paul Valery, his executors - given what follows, it is essential to stress the second and not the third syllable of that word - discovered several notebooks, in which the writer had jotted down, as they occurred to him, ideas for stories he would never write. Scholars, both disciples and detractors, have perused these notebooks with all the resources that their prejudices about the author would allow, and have proven, in their biographies and exegeses, that he was precisely the image of themselves projected upon his person that they had set out in the first place to describe. Such is the nature of literary criticism.

In Notebook 8, page 69, Valery himself questions the nature both of literature and of literary criticism, and goes on to dismiss as irrelevant any correspondence between the life of an author and his work - an argument completely, perhaps deliberately, undermined by a lengthy description of the adored professor who first taught him this idea, and of the arguments he had, to prove this view of literature, throughout his childhood with his father.

In Notebook 14, page 137, Valery offers this paragraph, which like so many of his notions was sadly never worked up into a full tale:

"Perhaps a short story about a man obsessed with the idea of killing somebody? He chooses a victim, plots and plans the murder, prepares to carry it out. As we read, we are appalled. His enjoyment of the detail (blood oozing, dismembered joints) affronts our sensibilities. His mental agility in constructing so elaborate a scheme reminds us of the warped imaginings of Sade and Moriarty. The story would contain innumerable red herrings, designed to fascinate the reader by their intellectual cleverness, and thereby lure them into the trap of liking and respecting this otherwise deranged man. So he goes out into the night, armed and resolute. So we witness the moments before the killing, and we, the reader, are brought to the very edge of our own selves, recognising our own darkest capacities within this vile man, yet also willing him on.

"And what if the name of this man were not Christie or Sweeney Todd, but Von Stauffenberg?"

THE GARDEN

Imagine a garden (Earl Jellicoe imagined precisely such a garden at Galveston) which cross-breeds all the great pedigrees of civilisation, a hybrid of all the world's great gardens, undertaken not for scientific nor aesthetic nor even archaeological purposes, but simply to expand the borders of the art of landscape gardening. In one area, the terraced hillsides of Tibet, cut off from the remainder of the garden by high mountains and vast tracts of desert; in another stands a terebinth, and in the pool beside it nymphs can be seen dancing; in a third, the hanging gardens of Babylon have been re-created, adjacent to those of the Tuilleries; a fourth is crossed by the four sacred rivers of Islam; a fifth hosts the World Tree, complete with Wotan's spear; elsewhere a Japanese garden in the style of Monet boasts a bamboo-and-lotus orchard dominated by a giant Buddha in the shadow of a pagoda; stones from Carnac and Zimbabwe are piled behind the cafeteria.

The gardens are more, far more extensive than described here; indeed, considering the presence of all known flora and the imitation of every known design, the gardens may - despite the finite space they occupy - be described as infinite. Egyptian and Mayan blend unobtrusively, Hispanic merges into Polynesian, Classical fuses with post-Modernist, even Jew and Arab stand unquarreling side by side. Yet sad to say, despite the abundance of temples, this is not a sacred garden, but a mere theme-park, subsidised by multi-national firms of seed and fertiliser and wheelbarrow merchants the better to advertise their wares.

Or perhaps the garden is sacred after all - if only to Mammon. Just as God - the universal gardener - may be no more than a metaphor, so here, too, has been carefully nurtured the supreme analogy. In this garden all paths are followed the same by all worshippers; this ingathering of the species generates a single culture which itself nurtures every species; harmony reigns supreme; God Is One.

THE BURNING OF THE BOOK

For weeks on end, the new priest had been struggling to fill his church, and even when he filled it, he struggled to gain the attention of what were less worshippers than participants in a social ritual. Women preferred to compare their hats with those of other women, rather than to heed the sermon. Men, too, gazed, lower than the women's hats, until they needed no priest to teach them the nature of sin. Only the weight of the collection box at the end of the service gave cause for satisfaction.

To bring these heathens back to God, then, a symbolic gesture was required, an act of faith. He would have preferred a miracle, but these are few and far between, and though he considered faking one, the danger of such an act outweighed its potential efficacy. No, a human gesture was required. To show these heathens the nature of their sins.

And so, taking advice from Paul and Augustine and Luther, he decreed the burning of the book.

Initially he thought to burn all books, those in the public library, those in the school-house, those too in the many private collections people had accumulated. But to burn all books is to condemn literature itself for witchcraft, and this was not his purpose. And besides, remembering the dialogue of God and Abraham at Sodom, there must have been at least some books which deserved not to be burned (though he couldn't himself have named any single one to support this sentimental idealism).

In the event, the priest decreed the burning of a single book, a symbolic book of wickedness, the vilest of them all, a book that enumerated and made manifest all the worst sins men were capable of perpetrating. The cursing of God. The making of bargains with the Devil. Rape. Murder. Incest. Torture. Adultery. Lasciviousness. Theft. Perjury. Abomination. The deliberate murdering of children. Regicide. The entire calumny of human sin.

So, that Easter Sunday morning - could any other morning have been so apposite? - the townsfolk gathered outside the church, where the pyre was already raised, and the flame already kindled.

So the priest committed to the fire, the last surviving copy in the world, of the book once called the Holy Bible.

DARWIN

In 1839, Charles Darwin, the "father of evolution", married his first cousin Emma Wedgwood. Both were of impeccable intellectual and social pedigree, but they were, nevertheless, first cousins, and Darwin's understanding of both Biblical and biological injunction should have served a double-warning.

The Darwins had ten children. Some were of marked scientific ability - there were even members of the Royal Society. Most, however, were sickly and delicate, the consequence, as we would now say, of genetic weakening and a thinning of the blood. Three died as infants. The last child, Charles Waring Darwin, was mentally deficient and died aged two, without ever learning to walk or talk.

I have quoted most of the above, practically verbatim, from Ben Macintyre's book "Forgotten Fatherland" (pp216/7). Macintyre poses, without perhaps even realising it, a number of immensely pertinent questions.

Did Darwin know about deleterious genes and the risk of cousinhood marriage - and if so, why did he allow love to outweigh wisdom?

Did the ancients - who knew how to breed in strains of speckles to otherwise white sheep - know about deleterious genes when they established their laws of incest?

Was Darwin consciously experimenting?

And does his own family serve as proving testimony to the Darwinian Law of Evolution, the so-called "survival of the fittest"? For if it does, then the proof also serves as disproof, since the family has now died out.

THE MIRACLE IN THE SAND

In the Talmud (*Ta'anit* 23a) we can read how the people of Israel found themselves blighted by a terrible drought, that turned the rivers into wadis and drained the wells, until it seemed the southern desert would swamp the northern swamps and they too would be left deserted. The drought threatened to outlast Methuselah. That August the people came to the august Rabbi Choni Ha Magel (he who said that, if a man does not enjoy the society of his fellows, it's as if he were dead) and asked him to speak to God on their behalf, as he was so pious God could not refuse him.

At first Choni was reluctant to tempt further one who must already have been angry with his people or he wouldn't have sent so terrible a drought. He argued that speaking would be useless, as God doesn't take part in dialogues; that bartering and negotiating would be useless, as the destiny of Mankind had been written and could not be altered; but that all things must end, including droughts and the anger of God, and that perhaps he could force the compacting of time in order to bring the written destiny to a speedier conclusion.

"I will not ask God to end the drought," he said. "But I will ask Him to bring forward the time of the end that He has already decreed, and I will do so, arguing that the purpose of the drought has already been fulfilled, since if men were not thoroughly chastised by it, they would not have asked for my intercession in the first place. I will argue that the continuation of the drought will cause men to doubt God's mercy, but that the advent of rain will confirm their faith. This is a form of seduction which God has never yet been able to resist."

Rabbi Choni's method was idiosyncratic, to say the least. He drew in the sand a perfect circle - the Cabalists insist to this day that the perfect circle is one of several metaphors for God; though they freely admit that the perfection of a circle also adds up to nought - and sat inside it, insisting that he wouldn't leave the circle until God had fulfilled his request. August turned to September, the autumn festivals came and went, and there, six weeks later, he still was, fasting and praying and near to death. In silence Rabbi Choni argued that a perfect circle represented both infinity and eternity, and that by placing himself within its limits (or strictly speaking its absence of limits) he could impart some influence upon time and thereby, himself, perform the miracle of compacting time and bringing to an end the drought. It was, he knew, a vain hope, but one that demonstrated to the world his piety.

For week after week he struggled, apparently in vain. And then, one morning, when Rabbi Choni lay parched and sick and dying, his friends came to ask him to leave the circle and to abandon the struggle. And whether because it was October, or because he had at last succeeded in engendering the miracle, or simply as an act of divine mercy and compassion towards the pious, dying Rabbi; whatever the explanation, on the morning after *Shemini Atseret*, in the last week of October, God sent the rain.

THE IMPERIAL MESSAGE

For F.K.

Ten thousand miles away in a city of gold stands the palace of the Emperor. Its walls are of porphyry and marble. Its chandeliers cast daylight and its mirrors duplicate the sun. By fountains that sprinkle liquid gold, the most gorgeous women in the world offer themselves as living statuary. Palm trees grow indoors. Arched vaults and vaulted arches complement each other, combining to manifest the genius of a thousand architects who have dedicated a thousand years to designing and redesigning the palace until it is perfect now in every way.

In the throne-room sits the Emperor. The lesser thrones to his right and left are occupied by the Empress and the Heir-Regent. Chamberlains, ambassadors, scribes and courtiers perambulate below the dais, waiting to be summoned. On a raised platform, a choir sings the courtly liturgy in gentle contralto, to the accompaniment of an orchestra of lutes. Ladies-in-waiting offer drinks and canapés on silver trays to dignitaries in clothes of ermine, silk and satin. There is an ambience of flawlessness, in the studied faces, in the pace of life, in the very surroundings. All who inhabit this realm understand that it is as close to Heaven as may be achieved on Earth. At its centre, the enthroned Emperor sits serene.

It is now that the third chamberlain notices the scantest movement of the third finger of the Emperor's left hand. Immediately he is at his liege's side. The chamberlain leans close to the Emperor's mouth, and receives the message. He nods. He looks at the Empress, whose smile confirms that she approves it. He looks at the Heir-Regent, whose nod likewise consents. The third chamberlain bows and leaves the dais. He whispers the message to the second chamberlain, who bows to the Emperor. He whispers it to the first chamberlain, who does the same. He approaches the door, summons a guard, and passes on the message, requiring its repetition to be sure there is no accidental alteration, for this is a message from the Emperor, and not a chinese whisper. The guard takes the message to the imperial envoy, and likewise requires repetition. The envoy summons a horse and rides away. So the journey of the message is begun.

The envoy rides a hundred miles, until his horse is tired, and passes the message like a relay-baton to a new envoy with a fresh horse, requiring the repetition. The second envoy rides to the third, the third to the fourth, and each envoy requires the repetition of the message, and each envoy is, albeit only slightly, still shabbier, more unsophisticated, more poorly dressed, the rider of a slower, less thoroughbred horse than the envoy who preceded him. After nine thousand nine hundred miles the message remains identical to that which the Emperor whispered, but the man who knocks at the door of your peasant hovel is the greengrocer's boy whose elder brother they hanged last Saturday for stealing horses, whose uncle ran away from that battle, for heroism in which the Emperor has now seen fit to honour you.

But surely the Emperor wouldn't send the greengrocer's boy to deliver news of such an honour; surely the Emperor wouldn't summon you to the palace on a horse whose ownership was so uncertain; surely the Emperor wouldn't honour anyway an obscure and unworthy peasant who lived ten thousand miles from the capital and whose heroism was in truth an act of simple human decency that surely anyone would have performed in the same circumstances? And so you curse the greengrocer's boy for being the nephew of a coward and the brother of a horse-thief, and you tell him to go and play his jokes on someone else, and slam the door.

AMANUENSIS OF THE SPIRIT

What is most remarkable amongst all the many virtues and attributes of the writer Jackson Abercrombie ("Famous Lives", the Trinidadian equivalent of "Who's Who", simply notes of him: *b P of Sp 6.3.27, editor, teacher, patron, author, d P of Sp 18.12.84*) is that this grandson of freed Dahomey slaves never actually wrote a single poem, play, essay, article or story in his life, and yet, perhaps paradoxically, is now regarded as one of the major literary figures of his day, in the Caribbean especially, but also well beyond. His influence upon Carridas and Chanderpaul, on the back-to-Africa "Anancism" movement, his role as editor and as mentor to both J.C. Nyland and Brian Ray, the immense importance of that absurdly named literary review "blahblah", and his strenuous patronage of any number of literary foundations, prizes, colleges and institutions across the Afro-Caribbean world, ensure that posterity will recall with gratitude at least three of the four epithets in "Famous Lives", whilst the fourth - author - provides his ticket to the pantheon of the literary gods, where hopefully they will let him in, despite his being, first, black, and, second, unpublished. Of his own writings, there are left behind only the ungerminated seeds - a single notebook which testifies to the plethora and eclecticism of his ideas, but which ought to infer a life's literary failure and the certainty of oblivion. Yet in truth it confirms the opposite. The notebook contains, in total, just the following:

1. Story of a king who goes mad with guilt and leaves his people to their own devices. The people carry on regardless and it becomes clear that the king was always irrelevant. Tell how they organised without the king.

2. Story of a rape which begins, "I had been a sick man most of my life, but now I'm whole again; had I not been fully cured, I could never have written this book."

3. Brechtian poem about the power of crowds etc, in mock verse, each stanza ending "while (when, why etc) Momma Poor saluted at the rally".

4. Story of a king who goes from land to land seeking a throne but fails to find one – "I have chosen you to be my people, this land to be my land" - they laugh and reject him - eventually some nomads accept him for their king, build him a litter and carry him with them wherever they go.

5. Hear about a marvellous person who is coming to visit; as different people impart more information about him, so the anticipation of

friendship turns from love to jealousy, betrayal etc - finally hatred and the fantasy of violently murdering him and butchering the body. "What pleasure I felt when this dreadful monster cancelled his visit."

(This piece is unique in that Abercrombie did actually write the opening paragraph, albeit with a change of gender. It goes as follows: "When Srinatha wrote to say that she was coming to Trinidad, and asked if she could pay us a visit, the delight on my face was palpable. I had already heard so much about her, had seen her fertile, fecund, smiling eyes on television, had read her pieces in the press. Who more beautiful, who more intelligent, who more exciting a prospect for a visitor than Srinatha?" What is particularly interesting about our having this example of Abercrombie's writing is the immensity of the gap between the idea and the execution. If this thoroughly indifferent sample is anything to judge by, we can state without fear of correction, that Abercrombie would have been a far less significant author *had he actually written any books*.)

6. Story of the enthroned but ignored king entitled "The Truth About Babel". God doesn't need to interfere - committees, sub-committees etc run and ruin everything - Torah replacing God as centrepiece of Judaism - God irrelevant...

7. Dialogue between the lapsed and the apostate Moslem, based entirely on non-Quranic scriptural quotations (Bhagavad Gita, Kapingamarangi, Book of the Dead, Analects); they argue about the nature of the deity in whom neither of them believe...the method is Socratic, the ideas amalgamate and synthesise Lao Tse and Aquinas.

8. Bartleby as an act of defiance, not negation; modern story along the same lines of a man who says no?

9. Trace the journey (evolution) of an idea, spawned in the mind of God, until today - changing like algae into Man, travelling along a spatial as well as a temporal path...

What is most remarkable about this list is not the absolute failure to turn any of the ideas into stories (his protégé Chanderpaul always insisted, after all, that the ideas were of greater value than the stories themselves since no tale could ever do full justice to a great idea), but the sheer immensity of Abercrombie's range. One can easily imagine a composer influenced by Brahms *and* Beethoven, by Mahler *and* Berlioz, but surely not by Debussy *and* Lutoslawski; similarly what painter could absorb such mutually exclusive influences as Giotto *and* Giacometti, as Frank Hubert *and* Franz

Hals, as Durer *and* Magritte? Yet the ideas cited above syllogise, respectively, Swift, Nabokov, Brecht, Chatwin, Sade, Koestler, Shlomo Agnon, via Buddhism, Shinto, Akhenaton and Confucius, not to mention Socrates, Averroes, Lao Tse and Aquinas, and finally Herman Melville and Jules Verne, and do so with consummate ease.

The astute reader will, in addition, have noted the stylistic influence of Lawrence ("fecund", "fertile"), the spiritual influence of Proust ("I had been a sick man all my life") and, perhaps not all that surprising for one brought up a Rastifari, a strong if negative affinity for both the Jewish and the Moslem. Also note the similarity between the first idea (a king goes mad so the people have to rule themselves), the third (which deals with the dangers of the democratic power of the mob), the fourth (the people who choose to be ruled by a king), the sixth (a king who is ignored by the people), and the seventh (the word of the heavenly king is argued by the representatives of the people), of which the most extraordinary thing that one can say is that, whilst in themselves the root ideas are entirely devoid of correspondence, could not know of each other, indeed were written in some cases several centuries and thousands of miles apart, in different languages and cultures, for a different audience; in Abercrombie's hand, by contrast, they become mere tedious repetitions of an increasingly obvious theme (and indeed so repetitive is the theme that we must ask ourselves whether ideas two, five, eight and nine are not also, in some way, variations.)

I end this note with a query, and ask my readers if any of you can throw light upon it. At the back of Abercrombie's notebook, in a hand that clearly isn't his own, the following two paragraphs appear, though it isn't evident whether and how they are related. Did Abercrombie disguise his own handwriting, and if so why? Did he perhaps dictate the two paragraphs to his secretary? Or are they not his at all, and if not his, then whose, and when, and why, and are they intended seriously, or as a joke? The first paragraph reads as follows:

"I am very much struck in literature by the appearance that one person wrote all the books...there is such equality and identity both of judgement and point of view in the narrative that it is plainly the work of one all-seeing, all-hearing gentleman."

And the second:

"To a Fly drowning in a glass of egged Brandy & water/saved him/he flies from sugar to Flower to Grass, to Plate - but the other miserable Drowning Man, the *Sot* the Drinker of the egged Brandy???"

THE JUDENRAT

Idea for a pun on the Judenrat[1]. Tell the story of a man trapped in the ghetto by the invading Nazis. Hiding in the cellar he hears the soldiers' conversation, and so powerful is the metaphor in which all of them believe, without doubt, with perfect, absolute and unswerving faith, that he is able to transform himself into the living shape of that metaphor, to pop his head out of the cellar and then, in the full gaze of their credulous eyes, to escape across the space between their chairs, out the front door, down a drainhole into the sewer, and thence away to that unlikely freedom which is the privilege of the Judenrat.

---

[1] *In German a "rat" is a council or committee, and the Judenrat was the Council of Jewish Elders in the ghettos, appointed by the Nazis to administer both the ghettos and the selections. It was perceived - wrongly as it transpired - as a means by which Jews might survive deportation and extermination. For further information, see the tale "Boruch Praszkier" in my collection "Tall Tales and Short Stories".*

THE THEFT

It is, everyone agrees, the most magnificent house - white-stone, early Georgian, porticoed. The interior decoration is by Charles Lasquallier, who came from New York to take personal charge. Not a room on all three storeys in which light does not hang from the walls like a painting by a great master, in which the most earnest thought has not been given to matching curtain materials to the texture of the furniture, or judging the voltage of the candle lamps to suit the nap and fibre of the parquet floorboards. A hundred years hence, the public will pay good money to experience the splendours of those parts of the mansion opened for its appreciation, and nod with admiration at such style, such taste, such opulence - such subtle eccentricity.

Eccentricity indeed! For what is most striking about the house is its complete resistance to - some might even say its rebellion against - the cultural *zeitgeist*. On all the walls of the house not a single painting hangs, nor any sculpture stands on plinth or sill, nor any book upon what is in fact a house devoid of shelves. No means of playing music, whether on live instrument or pre-recorded disc. No art, no literature. In short, a total absence of aesthetics, save only in the furnishing and ornamentation, and this is of the finest: the beautiful apotheosis of utilitarianism. A house created for a man who had made his fortune out of industrial technology, and who wasn't short of courage in declaring publicly and repeatedly his avowed contempt for culture. Light made of steel. Curtains that open and close electronically. In each room a visitor might avail himself of the advantages of a complex network of computers. Modern in every degree except its shell, the house was born in the Georgian epoch, but now it inhabits cyberspace.

What neither the computers nor the pet alsatian dogs could achieve, however, was the prevention of a highly determined burglar from entering and pilfering the house. Who he was remains unknown, for his crime was neither reported nor discovered. Shoeprints in the flower-beds behind the house suggest a lightly-built man of not more than medium height; a single strand found on the hinge of the window through which he entered show him to have been chestnut-haired, and in his early thirties. The shoes were probably trainers; the hair may have been dyed. In a bathroom on the first floor, the tiniest drop of blood inferred that the man had cut himself while breaking the glass on the fire door to the basement; a further, smaller smear of blood on the front door handle demonstrated the arrogance with which he had made his escape in broad daylight.

According to the solicitors acting for the house's owner, the basement contained nothing of any value, and since nothing equivalent to the deduct on the insurance had been stolen or disturbed, the police were entirely happy to let the matter drop. No file was opened. The provisional forensic report was recycled. All further investigation was dropped. Someone had broken into the house, apparently stolen nothing but trinkets, then left by the front door. An eccentric crime, in an eccentric house. Perhaps the burglar only wanted to prove that the house wasn't impregnable. But in fact, this was not the case.

In fact, the basement did contain three items. A painting by the Dutch surrealist Van Huyck, purchased anonymously at a New York auction for three and a half million dollars. An illuminated manuscript of the Gnostic Gospels, handwritten in Anglo-Saxon by the monks of St Bede in Norfolk, probably in the latter part of the eleventh century, value inestimable. A first and only edition of the Complete Works of John Smalley, obscure contemporary essayist, self-published and quickly remaindered, of no value at all financially or academically, though sentimentally John Smalley liked to think his essays on such esoteric themes as "the sterility of modern culture" and "global securities" would survive and be admired for as long as would his house.

We are left to ponder the paradox of a man who publicly protested against art and culture, yet kept hidden in his basement two of its most valuable examples; on his book of essays, which refuted all his public posturing; on how a burglar managed to assail that abode made otherwise impervious by electronics; on whether John Smalley's refusal to allow the police to investigate was to protect his reputation with his friends or his credit with the taxman; and why, having so successfully penetrated to the core of that resplendent house, the burglar made away, not with the monkish manuscript nor even the prized Van Huyck, but only the worthless book of essays?

THE EMPEROR'S GARDENER

Gardening was an act of therapy. After forty years of permanently secretarying in the offices of the royal treasury, retirement with a small pension and the part-time occupation of third assistant keeper of the royal roses was at once a sinecure and a panacea (the emperor's gardener liked to make such puns, while testing the mettle of his secateurs against the drier spears of second and third-year shoots.) If his back and thighs were no longer muscular enough to turn the compost heap or spread the mulch, still there was no one could outdo his capacity for picking just the right breeds to graft, one stalk upon another, in order to defy God by adding yet one more new rose - and the name of yet one more new rose - to the totality of Creation. The yellow butterfly rose, for example, which seemed too thin ever to take upon the stem of such a gnarled and stumpy wild garnet, and one so red into the bargain. Yet two years on, there was the most exquisitely speckled yellow ever. The Empress herself had commented on the delicacy of its fibres. And as to his pink and orange floribunda!

The Emperor's gardener loved especially the deep fleshy texture of the tea roses, and liked to see in their brief epiphany - barely a week from bloom to fading in some cases - a metaphor for life itself.

He loved to heal the sick roses. There were so many pests, both fungoid and invertebrate, it required the skills and training of an apothecary. Blackspot, leaf-cutting bees, moth-caterpillars, leaf-hopper fungus, rose rust, snails. The Emperor's gardener knew remedies for all of them.

He loved to design the patterns of the rose-beds, setting climbers and ramblers against the walls and pergolas, intermixing bush and shrub roses, decorating space with the most exotic blends of colour and a rueful playfulness of names. A Red Devil between a Josephine Bruce and a Royal Highness. A Silver Jubilee adjacent to a King's Ransom. A Danse du Feu next to a Swan Lake. The permutations were incalculable.

He loved to transplant wild buddleia from the royal woods - it seemed to grow with such infinite fecundity, to seed itself in every likely and unlikely place, just as did the lemon balm, the cuckoo pint - just to see if he couldn't induce butterflies into areas of the garden they had never previously explored. He loved to plant nut trees - the leggy hazelnut cobs, the stubbier almond trees - simply because of the birds who came down in the spring to feed on them.

Gardening was an act of therapy, both for God's impaired Creation, and for the weariness of his own age and spirit. And right now, therapy was precisely what the Emperor's gardener needed, for he was, at heart and soul, a deeply worried man. Not about the fungus on the blooms of the miniature rosinas, though this too was a matter of some concern. He was worried about his youngest grand-daughter, who had taken up recently with a young man of - the gardener didn't like to pass judgements, but in this case it was really unavoidable - questionable honour. The girl was openly discussing marriage, as though he had already asked her, as though her parents could be pressed into acceptance by its being made a fait accompli. Did she not know the boy's reputation? Was she naive to such a degree that she couldn't see the seducer behind that exterior of innocence and charm? And such long hair. And the dirt beneath his fingernails - no one had ever seen the Emperor's gardener at supper with his fingernails so grimy, not even after a whole day's gardening.

So the Emperor's gardener pruned, and frowned, pruned, and brooded. So he prized open the secateurs, set the blade horizontal on the flesh of a single rose, and delicately scraped the merest molecule of fungus from its surface. So he looked up into the shadows that had passed across his face, looked up automatically, as one does who is engaged upon a difficult and important task, and yet also deeply distracted. So he saw the Emperor walk by with his train of courtiers and sycophants. So he was staggered to hear his own voice, usually so taciturn in its respectfulness, so shy and dignified, laughing almost raucously that the Emperor was naked.

MYSTERIUM

Alexander Scriabin is remembered, by those who do, as the father of Russian Symbolist music, an idiosyncratically atonal music inspired by Chopin, though it seems unlikely that the master would have enjoyed it. Moscow-based for much of his life, he spent two years in Paris with Diaghilev, but returned to Russia in 1909, to work on his magnum opus, the "Mysterium". In fact it was already begun in 1903, and would remain incomplete when he passed into immortality in 1915. This multi-media work, planned some time before that transmutation, was to have been performed in the foothills of the Himalayas, to last seven days, and to bring about Armageddon; it was, in the composer's own words: "a grandiose religious synthesis of all the arts which would herald the birth of a new world." Scriabin left 72 pages of sketches just for the prelude to the *Mysterium*, entitled *Prefatory Action*. One hesitates to use the word "Wagnerian" to describe the length of the remainder.

Scriabin planned that the work would be synesthetic, exploiting the senses of smell and touch as well as hearing. He wrote that: "There will not be a single spectator. All will be participants. The work requires special people, special artists and a completely new culture. The cast of performers includes an orchestra, a large mixed choir, an instrument with visual effects, dancers, a procession, incense, and rhythmic textural articulation. The cathedral in which it will take place will not be of one single type of stone but will continually change with the atmosphere and motion of the Mysterium. This will be done with the aid of mists and lights, which will modify the architectural contours."

I try to imagine the fulfilment of this remarkable ambition, the apotheosis of what Mahler called "absolute music": the entire range of the Himalayas filled, each musician on a different mountain-top, thousands of instruments, choirs of millions, performing the world-song in a musical language so bewilderingly atonal, so compositionally confused, that even God could not intervene to buttress the heavens against this ultimate assault.

IN THE GYMNASIUM

In the gymnasium, surrounded by huge arsenals of equipment that resemble nothing so much as the racks of Torquemada clad in vinyl, ribbed in steel - the "hamstring curl" which requires you to lie on your stomach, clinging to the machine like a raft, and pedal yourself away from oblivion; the "bench press", said to stabilise the hand and wrist and flatten the abdominals; the "pectoralis", which is also known as the "bicepalis", the "coraco-brachialis" and the "deltoidalis", a kind of metal straitjacket that squeezes and stretches you until you confess and repent your every ounce of flab, and swear your oaths of loyalty, fidelity and anorexity to Adidas, the Jesuit god of fitness. There is also the "adductor kick" - elsewhere called the "abductor kick", a devastatingly sinister error of typography - which involves extending the hip from the thigh in one direction while simultaneously balancing on the outer, middle and big toes of the second foot, the remaining digits being rested, one in the vertical, the other in the horizontal position. This exercise is said to be particularly beneficial to sufferers from dyslexia and threadworm.

You are advised to warm up beforehand and to cool down after-hand, much as the fakirs (with an "i" please, not an "e") do in Tantric Yoga; and must wear the traditional clan uniform of sweaty shoes, shiny vests, and shorts so skimpy they reveal the perfectly trained condition of the genitals. I was particularly impressed by a technique - dare one say a "ceremony"? - known as the "York Dumbell" method, from which I took myself to be exempt on the grounds that I do not come from York. Finally, may I point out that the "free weights" are not to be used by the under-18s, though presumably the "captive weights" may be (no, I do not know how a weight obtains its freedom). Such is the terror inspired by these monsters, children under 14 must be accompanied by an adult; children over the age of 14 - whether ten, twenty, thirty or more years over 14 is not stipulated - are deemed safe to enter alone.

So much exertion, just to hone a decaying body in vain hope to delay its inexorable putrefaction! Yes, but after it's all over, what joy, to go home, to settle down in comfortable bad posture on a back-destroying sofa, by a raging fire of poisonous carbon monoxide, with a can of iced Coke, a symphony on the radio, a good book in hand, and thus to do the same thing, but with less travail, to the ever-expanding musculature of the mind.

ARTIST IN RESIDENCE

Most people live in rented accommodation - some of it put up by the council, some of it privately owned. There are, of course, those who own their own homes, or think they do - the truth is, most of them share ownership with a mortgage company, and theirs is by far the smaller share. Metroland, Brookside or Victorian Terrace, they live the lives that people live who inhabit such abodes.

Everybody dreams of one day building their own house, a house sufficient to accommodate their parents and grandparents and their siblings, their friends and lovers, to contain their life's experiences, to expiate their sins and their omissions, to flesh out their remaining dreams. Few are they who ever actually achieve it, and it may not be much when they do, but it's a house, and it's theirs, and it's an achievement truly worthy. And some of them build it once, but are unsatisfied with their own work, so they build it again, and then again, always the same house, the same life, but sometimes they add on or remove a room, sometimes they plant out or pave over a patch of garden, sometimes they build in wood instead of brick. But it's always essentially the same house.

There are other kinds of builders too. There are the municipal architects, the ones who are determined to leave behind a monument of public benefit, a town hall or a community centre, an edifice of cultural significance - Herr Schiller, for example, who established the library of rare scholarship, Monsieur Manet who opened the Japanese Garden, Comrade Shostakovich, who set up the cenotaph for the dead of the Great Patriotic War, Dr Freud who added a new wing to the hospital. There are the religious builders too, dedicators of private chapels, covenanters of whole churches, men and women who have their names engraved on silver plaques above the doors of churches, synagogues, meeting houses, mosques.

Most people live in rented accommodation. But there are the few, like Herr Mahler, or that Australian gentleman Mr White, or that strange American Bill Faulkner, who dedicate their lives to the single-handed construction of whole cathedrals. I myself dream of rebuilding the Temple in Jerusalem. But alas it isn't given.

THE CONFERENCE OF NOBODIES

The conference took place in one of those smart modern hotels which, unable to fill their rooms with travellers and tourists, have converted their facilities to meet the needs of training that community of amateur professionals who mismanage most of our national institutions. Two large rooms provided meals and plenaries, several smaller rooms were available for break-out sessions, and for two full days we worked with earnest intensity to learn the fashionable buzz-words which had replaced the fashionable buzz-words we learned three years ago, at the previous conference.

So we spent the first morning, setting, monitoring, reviewing and finally evaluating targets. After a pause for coffee we each laid out, on flip-chart sheets in primary school colours, our visions and our values. In the afternoon we undertook a base-line assessment of our personal effectiveness within the context of our institution's corporate performance, and that first evening we debated, in an enabling and mutually facilitating manner, first the difference between strategic planning and strategic development, then the difference between Base Value and Opportunity Cost, and finally the difference between philanthropy and patronage. It was all extremely fascinating.

On that first morning, each of us had shared with the group his or her first name, and pinned a first-name label to our smart lapels - I keep repeating the word "smart" to myself, because this, in the form of an acronym, was the buzz-word most deeply impressed upon our long-term memories, and by repeating it I hope eventually to stir my short-term memory into recalling what the acronym is meant to stand for. On the second morning, sadly convinced that I was no longer an active stakeholder in this fatuous training bunboree, I passed the time in learning and writing down the surnames of my colleagues, thinking that the networking, at the very least, might one day offer corporate advantage. I don't suppose that anybody else noticed what I noticed. It was, after all, just a list of names. Yet it made the most extraordinary coincidence. I attach the list in full, exactly as I learned it, and with absolute assurance to my reader that not a name have I made up. It reads as follows:

Charlie Dickens, Managing Director, Newgate Works Ltd
Ed Windsor, Senior Sales, Windsor Homes PLC
William Ockham, Marketing Manager, Gillette
Francesca Palgrave, Senior Partner, Meyer Cohen, Stockbrokers
John Murry, Solicitor, Mansfield & Middleton
James Cardigan, Public Relations, The Woollen Knitwear Co Ltd

John Stubbes, Personnel Manager, Gaping Gulf Travel
Matilda Tilley, Director, The Great Little Tilley Co
Bernard Montgomery, Project Co-Ordinator, Operation Victory
Anne Grant, Senior Sales, Highland Whisky Distillers
Andrew Jackson, President, The Horseshoe Bend Company of Tallapoosa (USA)
Gary Mercator, Regional Manager, Ordinance Survey
Liz Tudor, Artistic Director, Queen's Theatre Company, Hatfield

If these names and their employers continue to perplex you, may I strongly recommend that you take a dictionary of biography with you, next time you are compelled to endure one of these gratuitous conferences, and pass the time more usefully resolving the riddle of the list.

THE PRISONER

He dreamed, as all men dream, of liberty - the freedom to travel where and when he pleased, across time as well as space; yet how could he fulfil that dream, confined as he was, locked in so small a cell, of so closely guarded a tower, on such a fortress of an island, with nobody to talk to but the silent warders, and nothing else to do to pass his time than to work his way, book by book, through the infinite shelves of the prison library?

THE THEFT

The story of the burglary at the home of John Smalley, in August 1972, has already been recounted. New information, however, allows us to reconsider some of its detail.

In February 1976, the London auction house Sotheby's offered for sale a portrait of two children - probably the nieces of the 14th Viscount Latimer - with their governess - name unknown - and a magnificent Beadle Collie of russet hair and ears, the shape of dew-drops according to an amusing error in the catalogue, (we can presume "dewlaps" was intended); a diary entry of the Viscount's sister suggests this may have been Gwion, the sheepdog Howard Latimer trained to respond to instructions in both Welsh and English. The painter was Rodger Herrick, a pupil of Whistler and a friend of the disgraced poet Chatterton. Bidding commenced at the reserve price of two hundred and fifty thousand pounds. Several men in grey suits, located in different corners of the room, served as emissaries for a series of ornate telephones. The painting was bought, anonymously, for six hundred and ninety thousand pounds. Tabloid journalists who tried to pursue the delivery van in order to acquire the name of the new owner for their circulation war, were cheated by a complicated ruse involving dummy vans, an empty packing case on a DC11 jet, and two hoax phone-calls over the ensuing weeks. This labyrinthine strategy endowed the owner of the painting with perfect anonymity and the conviction that the work had crossed the Atlantic. The newspapers continued for years afterwards to lament the loss of such a major British work of art and to call for legislation to prevent its repetition.

Then, in June 1988, the industrial technologist John Smalley returned home to find police conducting forensic research into a burglary, and again informed them that, since nothing of any value had been stolen, he did not wish the matter pursued. The police withdrew. Household servants returned to the banality of their duties, and to their contractual obligation of public silence. John Smalley retreated to the now empty basement, wondering only if it were the same or a different burglar, and stayed there. It was said that this episode brought on the first of his strokes, the last of which would kill him.

The third incident in our story took place in May 1989. A telephone call to the National Gallery in London offered as an anonymous donation, in perpetuity and without conditions, a painting by the Dutch surrealist Van Huyck, an illuminated manuscript of the Gnostic Gospels, handwritten in Anglo-Saxon by the monks of St Bede in Norfolk, probably in the latter part of the eleventh century, and the Herrick portrait that continued to arouse so much indignation in the world of Art. Given the cost of preserving what was anyway a contentious manuscript, given the recent collapse of the reputation of Van Huyck, the first two offers were declined. The Herrick may now be viewed in gallery thirty-nine, alongside a pair of elegant portraits in miniature by Burne-Jones. A plaque beneath it states simply "Private Collection", without volunteering whose.

As to John Smalley. We continue to ponder, as we did before, all manner of whys and wherefores that comprise the character of a most eccentric man. But now there's something more, a human tragedy. For we are also left with the portrait of a helpless man, framed in the darkness of a private vault, gazing out of the empty nothingness that was once Creation, counting his losses, not in terms of Art, which he despised, but Capital.

TWO LEGENDS OF HITLER

According to the first legend, the Devil appeared to Hitler in a dream and made him this offer:

"For yourself you will receive nothing; you will fight on my behalf, and die, and your name will be cursed for ever. But to your children, and to your children's children, I shall give my kingdom in its entirety, the seas and the earth and everything that lives above, upon and underneath."

"What must I give in exchange, besides my life, which in the end I must lose anyway?" Hitler asked.

And the Devil replied:

"Do you recall how, in the Garden of Eden, I made this same offer to your ancestors Adam and Eve? In those days my price was one apple; today it has increased. Out of the multitude of souls that live, you will find for me and give me twelve million."

According to the second legend, it was the Almighty who appeared to Hitler in a dream and made him this offer:

"For yourself you will receive nothing; you will fight on my behalf, and die, and your name will be cursed for ever. But to your children, and to your children's children, I shall give my kingdom in its entirety, the seas and the earth and everything that lives above, upon and underneath."

"What must I give in exchange, besides my life, which in the end I must lose anyway?" Hitler asked.

And the Almighty replied:

"Do you recall how, in the land of Canaan, I made this same offer to your ancestors Abraham and Isaac? In those days my price was one ram; today it has increased. Out of the multitude of souls that live, you will find for me and give me twelve million."

Which of our children's children will learn the truth?

Who will foot the bill of their inheritance?

KERENSKY

There can be little disagreement that the Communist revolution in Czarist Russia, leading as it did to so many other Communist revolutions around the world, was one of, perhaps the most significant event of the entire twentieth century. And yet, what characterises the Communist revolution more than any other feature, is its total, abject, unequivocal and universal failure.

In some countries - Germany, for example - the revolution failed at its inception, or it was driven to destruction - as in the case of Chile - defeated by a Capitalist military machine (so runs the ideological language of its propaganda) that was backed, indubitably, by the forces of the International Zionist Conspiracy (Jews, you will note, are the traditional scapegoats for all sides in these conflicts; Kerensky, you will note, like Leon Trotsky, like Karl Marx himself, was Jewish).

In other countries - Italy, say, or Ethiopia - it failed by imploding inwardly, one Communist cell in dispute with another, until the structure simply fell away. Elsewhere - the Israeli kibbutzim, for instance - it failed by becoming an anachronism, no longer relevant to the social and the economic conditions that came to prevalence precisely because of its initial success. Similarly in China, in Cuba, in Nicaragua, each in its own way, the revolution failed because its own success turned it, paradoxically, into an image of the very enemy it had come into being to destroy - pigs and men, as Orwell fabled it, grown indistinguishable. Some countries took longer than others, and several retained the name long after they had abandoned the ideology, but today, as I write, in 1997, on the eightieth anniversary of the Revolution which Kerensky led, there remains no country in the entire world that can genuinely describe itself as Communist. Insofar as Communism is concerned, the twentieth century was an experiment which failed. Be grateful there are an infinity of centuries.

The failure of the revolution is mirrored in the story of the premier revolutionary. The very first Communist to rule a country of his own was Alexander Kerensky, born at Simbirsk - now Ulyanovsk - the son of a headmaster[2]. A lawyer by training, Minister of Justice in March 1917, Minister of War in May, Premier in July, victor over Kornilov in the revolt of September, he was deposed by the Bolsheviks in November 1917. From revolutionary to exiled leader in just nine months - the gestation period of a stillbirth, you might say. Why, even Che Guevara lasted nearly two years before the Bolivians finally gunned him down!

[2] It may interest the reader to learn that, amongst the students under Fedor Kerensky's headmastership, was Vladimir Ilyich Lenin.

What happened to Kerensky after his deposition? Where does the leader of a Communist revolution go, when other Communists have declared him a reactionary, a revisionist, a traitor to the cause, an anti-Communist? His books describe the coda of his life, in descending scale, like a political arpeggio. In 1919 he wrote "Prelude to Bolshevism"; in 1927 he chose for a title the unambiguous "The Catastrophe"; eight years later, in 1935, desuetude was even more embedded, when he called his third book, "The Road to Tragedy". Whether personal and Communistic, or simply personal, or simply Communistic, the title does not give away, but tragedy it certainly was, and not only for Kerensky. All these books were written in France. But in 1940 the French too declared him unwelcome (the Vichy French, for whom the Jew Kerensky was simply one more Jew, indistinguishable from other Jews whose political affiliations were equally irrelevant, saved from the Nazi ovens only by his notoriety), and he sailed to the safe haven of Australia, remaining in that distant outpost of civilisation until civilisation at the centre had ceased to tear itself apart.

Then, in 1946, when the Marshall Plan announced the beginning of the Cold War, Kerensky joined the enemy, remaining in the enemy camp until he died, in 1970, having spent those twenty-four years teaching the history of the 20th century, a subject about which he patently understood extremely little but which included his own name in the frontispiece, at the University of Stamford, in the USA.

ST JUDAS OF THE HOLY BETRAYAL

For H.J

Already they are celebrating the close of His second millennium, and still the fools, the fools have never understood.

To save the world He had to be immortal.

To be immortal He had to be resurrected.

To be resurrected He had to harrow Hell.

To harrow Hell He had to die in agony.

To die in agony, real, public, visible agony, so that there was no doubt about the fact of His mortality, in those days there was only crucifixion.

But a man cannot offer himself for crucifixion, and a prophet of Truth and Honesty and Justice cannot commit a sin sufficiently heinous to be arrested, charged and sentenced. Someone had to artifice it. Someone had to make it possible. His mission was to be the Azazel, the scapegoat who carried all our sins away upon His back. But how could He be the paschal lamb if no one took Him to the Temple to be sacrificed?

He chose me - me! - because there was no other among the disciples who He trusted to perform the deed. They would have shied away, those doubting Thomases and thrice-denying Peters. They would have tried to persuade Him to give five shekels to the High Priest in His place, to make the *pidyon ha ben*, the redemption of the first born. They would have slunk into oblivion rather than - rather than what? - rather than committing what they ignorantly thought was a betrayal? But it was no betrayal. It was an act of fulfilment. It was a divine necessity. It was a prerequisite for consummation. It was the holy act that made possible His divinity. It was the raising of a son of man to the status of a Son of God. What act more holy in all history?

And if I took my own life, if I hanged myself from a tree in a field, it was not remorse, nor shame. That's simply the foolish presumption of those who fail to understand my role. Why should I feel remorse, why shame? Was I not given the second greatest part in History, like the angel at Penuel who was chosen to wrestle all night long with Israel? No, it wasn't shame, it was self-disgust. To think that I had taken money, Roman money, for doing what I would happily have done, should happily have done, for free.

THE DISPUTE

The dispute had raged for generations. On the surface it seemed a simple enough matter, but the fact was, it had divided the community, torn it apart, separated whole families, broken up businesses, made enemies of former friends - much as the Big Enders had been divided from the Little Enders and the followers of Hillel from those of Shammai. At times the dispute had been carried on in an orderly though always combative manner - depositions presented at the Rabbinical Court, public disputations by the learned, tracts and treatises published in Yiddish newspapers or university journals. At other times, however, the matter descended into imbroglio, bickering and even fisticuffs - Rabbi Joshua the Maggid received a black eye in the very lobby of the Yeshiva, Rabbi Yitschak the Mitnaged had three ribs broken when he was set upon one evening, en route to express his opinion on the matter in a Yom Tov sermon.

Those who had read the texts of the goyim said it was like the dispute between the Capulets and Montagues, and that it needed a Prince, or at the very least a Rebbe, to order the dispute ended, on pain if necessary of excommunication. Yet how could such a dispute simply end? Was it not a matter of God's Law that was in contention? Did not the very way men lived their lives depend on it, for if the Law was misinterpreted - and both sides were adamant that the other was seriously misinterpreting it - then the soul stood in jeopardy through all eternity. Disputes, they argued, were both necessary and inevitable. Disputes gave a community its dynamism. And those who disagreed, disagreed.

In the town square, the Rebbe been summoned as their mediator held his hands up to the Heavens, and besecched the people to live in peace and harmony and give up their quarrel. But no one listened. One Rabbi shouted his opinion from one side of the market, another from another. Crowds of disciples cheered triumphantly, or bellowed at their rivals.

Then, suddenly, a miracle occurred. From out of the Heavens boomed a voice, the voice of God Himself, ordering the people to give up their dispute, to return to harmony, to make peace. At once, on all sides, enemy turned to enemy, rival turned to rival, and as one they came together, joined in confraternity against the unjust intervention of the King of Kings. How dare He, the Rabbis called in unison? How dare He, the townsfolk echoed like a *responsum* to a prayer? How dare He, Almighty God, concern Himself with a dispute between Man and Man? He had done His part, centuries ago, when He gave the Law to Man through Moses. Interpretation wasn't His business. A dispute of interpretation lay in the province not of God but Man, and Heaven had no right to interfere. Everyone agreed. By evening, the town was at peace.

THE VULTURE

A man dreams a fearful image (I've chosen the word "fearful" very carefully, aware that it conveys precisely the idea that I'm trying to convey, and that similar but different words, such as "frightening" or "nightmarish", would be inexact). A man dreams a fearful image. He doesn't conjure up this image from his imagination, nor does he retrieve it from his memory, for he's operating in the realm of dream, not literature. It's an image that manifests itself inside his dream, a function of the act of dreaming. That's to say, he dreams, and because he's in a state of anxiety, a vulture (but it could have been any creature, real or fictitious; I've merely chosen to suggest the possibility that it was a vulture) swoops down upon him, threatening to tear him limb from limb and carry him away.

The dream lasts seconds, or even less than seconds, but within the dream the moment of extreme terror is eternal. The vulture swoops eternally. Fear grips the dreamer eternally. The shaking of his threatened limbs goes on eternally. All conceivable anxiety is manifested and expressed, in this ephemeral moment and forever.

Yet the vulture neither tears nor carries him away, for inside the dream some resolution manifests itself which likewise the dreamer neither conjures nor recalls, but which too is a function of his anxiety and of his need to overcome it; as eternal as the vulture, but an eternality of healing.

When he awakens he recalls the dream as "a vulture nearly tore me limb from limb, but miraculously I survived" (like God the Pantocrator Himself, we require words to make and tales to explain our universe), quite unaware that both the vulture and the miraculous escape were merely chemical reactions, shapes his anxiety had taken, the one to make it manifest, and the other to resolve it.

THE MAN WHO MISSED EVERYTHING

Certain facts about his life may not seem quite so extraordinary once the reader gets beyond the title of this biography[Y], though Jocelyn Reynolds does Wintlock a great disservice by choosing so cruelly sardonic an epithet for his subject. Reynolds is thorough, meticulous and detailed, but like most biographers he imposes his self-image upon that of his subject, and we find ourselves too often wondering whose biography this really is.

Geraestus Wintlock, as we learn, was born on the little known Greek island of Pentheos (the name means "grief") in 1917, at a time when his mother's desperate illness (she came from a family of suicidal depressives) had persuaded his father to break free of European life and seek sanctuary and solitude as far away as possible from all vestiges of civilisation - Reynolds facetiously posits that he might have achieved the same result by remaining at his home in Blaenau Ffestiniog; this is the kind of unnecessary sarcasm that repeatedly undermines the scholarship of this elsewise worthy volume. When his mother recovered she took on his education, supported by a native ayah (native to India that is, where Joy Wintlock herself grew up), and he became completely conversant in several ancient languages and literatures, as well as in myth and history, although his knowledge of science extended little further than Averroes and Galen. Of the mediaeval and the renaissance he learned nothing (Reynolds observes that "he had not even heard of William Shakespeare"), and in truth he never would.

Wintlock's effective life began in 1938, when he accepted an invitation to take part in an anthropological expedition to the remote Polynesian island of Dukkah, where he spent eleven years seeking evidence of the existence of the anicca, a rare species of marsupial believed to have become extinct (and so it proved), as well as undertaking a major act of comparative mythology whose methodology (given that he had never read him and given his complete immersion in the ancients) may be said to have predated and predicted J.G. Frazer by some minus-fifty years. The outcome of this work was his *chef d'oeuvre*, "Ancestor Worship Amongst The Polynesian Aboriginals", published on his behalf in Rome in 1942. Wintlock in the meanwhile had taken up a post in Anatta in the Gujerat - his mother's birthplace - where he began his major study of the Sanskrit roots, through Phoenician, of the Greek and Hebrew tongues. Reynolds, sadly, omits the details of this undertaking.

Public appearances by Wintlock have been few and far between (one has the impression that he does not, and would not wish to own a television).

Ψ *"The Man Who Missed Everything; a life of Geraestus Wintlock" by Jocelyn Reynolds. The Argaman Press, 1999*

His appearance on the BBC television programme "Book Choice" at the weekend, inspired by Reynolds' need to sell his book, allowed us a rare glimpse of what is now a frail old man of eighty-two, so accustomed to solitude and to speaking Hindustani as to be virtually inarticulate in English. He spoke with great feeling about the plays of Aeschylus - the subject of his next book and described by him as "my favourite contemporary playwright" - and with great disappointment about modern attitudes to Pythagorean ethics; though his comments on the revival of the caste of the so-called "untouchables" in southern India did leave a sour taste, until one realised that he was referring to its revival in the 11th century.

Nevertheless, many reading Reynolds' book, and many watching that television interview, will have wondered at his out-of-touchness. He knew, literally, nothing of two world wars, let alone those of Vietnam and Yugoslavia, knew nothing either of the atom or the hydrogen bomb, had no notion that man had walked in space or on the moon, was oblivious to the impeachments of two American presidents, to the failure of quasi-fascism in Britain in the 1990s, of the Common Market or the United Nations, of the revival of Islam or the collapse of Communism. Not simply the 20th century, but all centuries from the 14th onwards, had quite simply passed him by. And yet, as he spoke - so wistfully, so serenely, like a contented Buddha - one could not help but feel that he was better off.

THE COURTESAN

Since the age of fourteen, when her grandfather and her great-uncle raped her, both at the same time, she had slept (she counted them, keeping a record of their names, of their qualities as well as their depravities, in a series of plain, school exercise books that she hoarded in a box beneath the floor) with one thousand nine hundred and eighty-seven men - though "slept with" is a considerable exaggeration ("life," she once famously observed, "is absolutely meaningless unless you exaggerate"), but also a figure of speech, since what had been involved was merely an ephemeral act of sexual congress, the gratification of one desire, the desire for sex, upon another, the desire for money.

Desire, however, was never fully gratified. Of those one thousand nine hundred and eighty-seven men, well over half had failed to obtain their objective - every man's objective with a woman is subtly different, but failure is always failure - while more than half of the remaining half had set out with ambitions so paltry and so limited that it was an insult to the name of courtesan to provide what they required - a mere caressing with the hands, a reciprocated grope and fumbling round the upper or the lower body, a series of hapless thrusts and hopeless grunts, culminating in a transitory and disappointing epidermal spasm. It all seemed so pointless, such a terrible waste of money, not to mention the far more terrible waste of passion and desire. And what of love? As they lay grunting on top of her, secretly watching her for signs of pleasure so that they could believe they were not faked, she planned her shopping expeditions or decreed the colour of the nail varnish she would wear on Saturday for some other man, or sometimes she amused herself imagining the real names of these men who had lied to her, as she had lied to them, about her real name.

After so many years of so many men, it was no longer the men, nor even the money with which they purchased momentarily the various orifices of her body, but the book of the men, and especially the planned denouement of that book, that now absorbed her. Even as they lay floundering and grumbling inside her, she found herself constructing sentences - some of them extraordinarily poetic, others as banal as journalism and as trite and trivial as sex itself - in which she would record the experience afterwards, mimicking in written words the actual words that they had used, seeking the *mot juste* with which to celebrate the absolute uniqueness of what was otherwise merely another gruesome replica of the universal male model.

So she would smile at her own wit and ingenuity, and the man would mistake it for his virility. So she would elevate sex to the level of art, and understood at last why the ancients regarded their hierodules as priestesses.

So she would go out on the streets, no longer willing to be taken by whatever man should happen to invite her, but seeking only certain men, those who conformed to the phrases she had determined in advance to write about them, seeking certain shapes of noses, colours of eyes, shades or textures in the hair or skin, tones of voice, even certain modes of copulating or preferences for the more bestial of acts.

So it was that she wrote her act of suicide, planned for the night of the 16th of August, the twenty-fifth anniversary of her initiation by her grandfather and her great-uncle. So it was that the perpetration of the act of suicide - an act of which the police have found no physical evidence, and which to this day is regarded in their files as a case of "missing persons" and not one of "unexplained mortality" - came to represent for her the ultimate and culminating sexual moment of her life. She would find two men, identical in every way to the men who had initiated her, and she would re-enact with them each moment of her rape. Then, at the instant when the two of them achieved orgasm - in the written account they did so simultaneously, though one suspects the hand of the creative artist not that of the courtesan at work here, inventing synchronicities that life itself, alas, rarely affords - each would receive the still greater liberation from the flesh that death provides. In the written account, a silver blade would disembowel them, one with her left hand, one with her right, and then the two blades would be drawn out again, and plunged into her own flesh. So, as she wrote, revenge would be complete (the words she used, somewhat heretically, somewhat romantically, were "*consummatum erat*"). And with revenge, justice.

What happened to her, what happened on that night, remains unknown, other than that she disappeared without a trace, and that on the self-same night two old men of the city disappeared as well. In her dingy, tawdry room, the police found nothing but a few belongings, and the book of her encounters, marked "*finis*" and neatly underlined, with the heading "August 16th – 1990" scrawled in the upper margin of the final page, a heading which the police initially misunderstood to be the date.

THE SAD CASE OF LAWRENCE OF ARABIA

T.E. Lawrence - Lawrence of Arabia - was of course a fraud, a charlatan, a fake. The extraordinary crossing of the Nefud to take Aqaba from the rear owed more to unseasonally inclement weather than to the human capacity to endure immeasurable heat. The unification of the Arabs wasn't achieved by a charismatic call to their idealism but by the unfulfilled promise of boxes full of gold. The Arab revolt against the Turks was really nothing but a sideshow, and took place only after the English had already driven the Ottomans out of Arabia. The famous incident at Daraa was almost certainly an invention. The vestments of a prince of the Charif were mere vanity - and rarely worn in life or action, no matter how often he posed in them for the benefit of news photographers. The detailed account of his campaigns, recorded so minutely in "Seven Pillars of Wisdom", was make-believe, retrospective wishful-thinking, fiction. The political visions he laid before Churchill and Sheikh Faisal were naive, unrealistic, unachievable. So say, anyway, the enemies of Lawrence of Arabia, those mean-spirited souls so bound by their own limitations that they cannot bear it that someone else threw off the shackles, and made himself a hero.

The truth is, all heroes fabricate their own legends, or else their disciples do it for them. George didn't really slay a dragon, Prometheus didn't literally steal fire from the gods, Jacob didn't actually wrestle with an angel, Jesus didn't physically raise the dead. The legends, the myths, the tales function at the level of metaphors, and human beings require such metaphors to make life palatable. And as much as they require metaphors, so too do they require heroes.

What is sad about T.E. Lawrence isn't that he fabricated so much mythology, that he was a false idol, that he had feet of clay. Leviathan was a false idol, the Sphinx had feet of clay - but neither is less magnificent for that. Whitman, the greatest poet of the modern age, did nothing all his life but fabricate the myth of Whitman, the greatest poet of the modern age - and therein lies his greatness and his failure. So, too, T.E. Lawrence.

But what is sad is none of this. Rather it's the way in which, given the opportunity to elevate a true hero to the pantheon of the gods, those mean-spirited creatures could only accommodate him by seeking every feasible means to debunk him, until the opportunity for hero-status was gone, until, as another Lawrence, D.H., put it, they had "missed their chance with one of the lords of life". In David Lean's film version there dwells a great and glorious hero for the modern age. But among certain human beings, alas, to become such a hero, one first has to be crucified. Even as I write these lines, the sound of the hammers is still audible, the smell of sponge and vinegar continues odoriferously to nauseate.

THE RAINBOW

For years I had argued that ghosts were only ever seen, like fairies and religious visions, by those who were preternaturally inclined, who already believed in ghosts and fairies and religious visions; and so, perhaps, I was more amenable to the experience I shall relate here than many another person might have been.

I first encountered the idea of the doppelganger - that curious blasphemy of God in which a double of oneself repeats oneself unparented - when I was a student at the university, devouring literature with the voracious hunger of a Moloch. I recall, for example, Dostoievski's strange tale "The Double", as well as several texts by Robert Louis Stevenson. There was also that minuscule paradox of Borges' in "Borges and I", which he later repeated virtually identically in "August 25th, 1983". And then more recently, a bewitching line in Naguib Mahfouz' story "The Time and the Place", where his "alter ego" (I dislike this translation from the Arabic; a "fetch" or "wraith" would have been more accurate) invited him to "accept the gift of a miracle", reawakened my curiosity without any genuine hope of satisfying it. And because I was intrigued - and what is inquisitiveness if not the agnostic pursuit of certainty? - so I had wondered, and imagined, what I might say and do should the implausible eventuality occur.

All this, as I say, took place in the esoteric realm of ideas, where so much exists that bamboozles and bewilders, that defies the credible - though never half so much so as does actuality itself. For what I encountered that afternoon - it was raining, as I recall, but strong sunlight on the far side of the mountain had caused the two ends of a rainbow to settle with quite startling beauty, one on either side of the flooded valley like the legs of the Colossus; echoed by a second, equally incandescent rainbow, which arched above it; and I was thinking as I stared at it of the covenant made by God with Noah, wondering whether a second covenant or a second God were not perhaps implicit in this extraordinary phenomenon, when...

What I encountered that afternoon, as I began to say, wasn't a doppel nor a trippelganger, but a full scale...what can one feasibly call such a phenomenon? Three images all at once, and clearly, visibly, indisputably, all of them - myself. Yet not I, the one who stood there watching them approach. A former self, a self yet to be, the third my mirror-image, ambling aimlessly across the hills - like Noah's sons, it did occur to me - out for some Sunday ramble and a chance to see the flooded valley in this space between rain and still more rain.

I was reminded of the riddle of the Sphinx ("What has four legs, then two legs, then three legs?"). But I have to admit that I didn't respond sympathetically to any of my alter egos. The young man looked surly and unpleasant, had a manner that was closed and secretive and somehow arrogant, and it tore at my heart and memory to think some Dorian Grayish trick were being played on me to punish me for being who I once had been. Yet even this was as nothing by contrast with my present self. A more abhorrent, a more detestable creature couldn't be imagined, so much so that I cannot even bring myself to write about him. But at least - and this revelation rendered the whole bizarre experience worthwhile, if somewhat disconcerting - at least I could discern a handful of redeeming features in the man whom I was yet to be: a source of hope, if nothing more than that.

They approached me - grandfather, father, son - seeming so absorbed in their own adventure that they didn't notice me. Or perhaps they didn't recognise me as their alter ego. Or perhaps, being ghosts of sorts, being enigmas and occult mysteries, being the illusory manifestations of ideas and not flesh and blood at all, perhaps they didn't see me because they didn't believe in me, or because to them I wasn't there. Slowly they approached me, passed me, walked on by me. I turned to follow them as they continued on their ways, but the vision of the double rainbow soon enough distracted me, and by the time I turned to look for them again they were long departed - vanished as it seemed - over the far brow of the hill.

CASANOVA

Since the age of fourteen, when his aunt and his governess seduced him, both at the same time, he had slept (he counted them, keeping a record of their names, of their virtues as well as their more enterprising vices, in a series of leather-bound, ornamented diaries that he stored in an oak-chest in his library) with one thousand nine hundred and eighty seven women - though "slept with" is a considerable exaggeration ("life," a certain courtesan he knew had once famously observed, "is absolutely meaningless unless you exaggerate"), but also a figure of speech, since it was rare indeed that he stayed a whole night in a woman's company, and if he did so, sleep was never a priority.

Men who enjoy food do not think of themselves as gluttons, any more than men who enjoy computers or trainspotting think of themselves as suffering from *anoraksia nervosa*; so he didn't think of himself as a Don Juan or a Casanova, but merely as a man who enjoyed sex, and who could see no more logic in monogamy than in always eating soft boiled eggs for breakfast. Nor was he averse to paying courtesans or even street-women for their sexual favours, on the perfectly rational grounds that no sexual favours were ever granted until a man had spent a sufficient sum of money, but that with a courtesan you could at least be certain that the woman you slept with was also the recipient of your cash. A whore, by contrast, was obliged to cede some large percentage to an undeserving pimp, while with a woman that you simply met and made love to, it passed entirely to florists, restaurateurs, theatre impresarios and hotel porters, not to mention the purveyors of jewellery, overpriced canal-boats, and rich chocolates.

Desire, however, wasn't always gratified. Of those one thousand nine hundred and eighty seven women, with well over half he had simply failed to obtain his objective - a man's objective is subtly different with every woman he encounters, but failure is never his failure - whilst with more than half of the remaining half he had set out with ambitions so paltry and so limited that it was an insult to the name of courtesan to ask them to provide what he required - a mere opportunity to caress with his hands those parts of a woman that had taken his passing fancy, an unreciprocated grope and fumbling round the upper or the lower body, a series of hapless thrusts and hopeless grunts, culminating in a transitory and disappointing epidermal spasm.

It all seemed so pointless, such a terrible waste of money, not to mention the far more terrible waste of passion and desire. And what of love? As he lay grunting on top of her, secretly watching her for signs of pleasure so that he could believe they weren't faked, he knew that she was planning her next shopping expedition or decreeing the colour of the nail varnish she would wear on Saturday for some other man, or in one case (he'd found the box of plain school exercise books she hoarded underneath the floor) amusing herself by imagining the real names of these men who had lied to her, as she had lied to them, about her real name.

So it happened that, for years and years, for all his life indeed since that day of his double initiation by his aunt and governess, not one day had gone by in which he hadn't coupled with some female (he attributed his mental health and physical longevity to it), whether in his imagination or in actual flesh, but that particular woman haunted him, for reasons he could never fathom, which he thought perhaps was her secret store of books that mirrored his own store, but which we can see was fate trying to reveal itself. For so eventually it did, years after their first encounter, when he was an old man who had gradually come to learn that really he was homosexual, as all men are really homosexual but need to pursue their own maleness through the female rather than through other males. But I'm digressing.

Years later, then, he met again this woman of the secret books, took her to bed again, imagined what he would write about her writing about him, wondered if she could or could not be counted as his one thousand nine hundred and eighty eighth; and so distracted was he by the strange phenomenon - one which, for all his libertine pursuits, he had never previously engaged in - of sharing a woman with another man, so preoccupied was he by the thought that life remained absolutely meaningless even when you exaggerated, that he completely failed to notice the silver dagger she was drawing from beneath her pillow, or at least by the time he did notice it was too late.

PROMETHEUS

In punishment for stealing fire from the gods and giving it to man, Prometheus was chained to a rock in the Caucasus, and eagles were sent to feed upon his liver, which was eternally renewed. Such was the nature of his crime that the punishment was decreed in perpetuity, and yet, despite my having travelled the length and breadth of the Caucasus, despite my having searched in every niche and nook and cave and cranny, I have been forced to resign myself to the fact that Prometheus is not there, the eagles are not there, the liver is not there, even the gods are not there. No, today there is only rock, the empty eyries of the eagles, the marks on the red stone that could be blood or iron or simply the erosion of the sandstone by the rains, the occasional bundle of embers blackening the surface of the rocks, the sighing of the breeze that wafts out of the ocean, bringing its merciful balm against such terrible hot sun. Yet in the deep valley I discovered - and who can say if this was by coincidence or not - the carcass of an eagle, the charred skeleton of a man, a piece of broken chain, a morsel of rotten liver, the loyalty of a people to a fire-god whose mercy is as eternal as his wrath.

THE UNWELCOME VISITOR

An earlier story in this volume, "Amanuensis of the Spirit", included a list of those ideas for tales that have contributed to making Jackson Abercrombie famous. Among them was this proposal:

"Hear about a marvellous person who is coming to visit; as different people impart more information about him, so the anticipation of friendship turns from love to jealousy, betrayal etc - finally hatred and the fantasy of violently murdering him and butchering the body. What pleasure I felt when this dreadful monster cancelled his visit.'"

This done, I then wrote that:

"This piece is unique in that Abercrombie did actually write the opening paragraph - albeit with a change of gender. It goes as follows: 'When Srinatha wrote to say that she was coming to Trinidad, and asked if she could pay us a visit, the delight on my face was palpable. I had already heard so much about her, had seen her fertile, fecund, smiling eyes on television, had read her pieces in the press. Who more beautiful, who more intelligent, who more exciting a prospect for a visitor than Srinatha?'"

Now, six years later, I offer my apologies for misleading my readers (though not, I hasten to add, for deceiving them, for deceit implies intent and I was as misled as anyone). I apologise, with even more remorse, to Srinatha Jarasayawa, the genuine author of "The Unwelcome Visitor", who has fought, and now won, a concerted battle in the law-courts of Trinidad to assert her right of ownership of this story, stolen as it now appears, much to the discredit of the Trinidadian literary establishment, and to the posthumous reputation of Jackson Abercrombie (the other reasons for his discreditment need not occupy us here; suffice it so say we were all as astonished as we were appalled by the recent revelations of wife-beating and debauchery).

Though Srinatha's authorship is no longer questioned, continuing appeals against the financial damages have rendered the tale *sub judice*, as a result of which it still cannot be published. No doubt, given the Trinidadian literary establishment's on-going support for Abercrombie even in spite of all the recent revelations, we have to presume that the story will remain *sub judice* for ever. It is therefore in the spirit of samizdat, solidarity, and opposition to all forms of censorship that I risk all to publish now, here and in cyberspace, what might otherwise be condemned to perpetuity in my tale "The Index".

Here is the original, dated December 1984:

THE UNWELCOME VISITOR

When Jackson wrote to say that he was coming to Trinidad, and asked if he could pay us a visit, the delight on my face was palpable. I had already heard so much about him, had seen his fertile, fecund, smiling eyes on television, had read his pieces in the press. Who more handsome, who more intelligent, who more exciting a prospect for a visitor than Jackson?

But then, that Thursday, at the library, I bumped into Dr Ramasingranati, who told me a strange story about Jackson, how he had come to Dr Rama's house to stay one time, and he had found him rummaging through the good doctor's notebooks, copying down ideas for stories.

"Yes," he told me, "and speak to Linton Matura. Not only did Jackson steal two of his poems and publish them in his magazine anonymously, he stole Linton's wife as well, and now he says he's going to marry her."

I knew Linton Matura's wife from my schooldays, so I rang her up, but to my surprise the only voice that answered was a maid's.

"The lady gone," she told me in her aspirated Bajan. "Taken all her tings and ran away she has. All dem tings he hasn't locked up in his attic so she couldn't get at dem, dat is. She at her mom's."

I rang Linton Matura's wife at her mother's, but there was no excitement about her forthcoming marriage, only the gory details of a beating which I thought she meant Linton Matura had given her; but no, it was Jackson who had beaten her till she was black and blue, Jackson who had tried to force her to commit the most unspeakable of acts, Jackson who had fed her koy carp to the jaguars as a way of punishing her, Jackson who had threatened to cut her with a razor when she tried to run away. We shared openly a desire to take violent revenge on him.

And he was due to visit me on Saturday! I telephoned my father to ask for his advice, but all he did was laugh, and then laugh more and more.

"It isn't funny dada," I kept telling him, but he wouldn't stop.

"Of course it's funny, you silly little girl. All dem stealings and beatings and cuttings - haven't you read this month's 'blahblah'? Everyting you told me's in a story there right now. It's a fiction, girlie. Dees tings never happen."

"You tink Linton Matura's wife be lying? You tink she just going along wid someting? I heard her voice. Dat weren't no goin' along."

My father laughed again and the phone went dead - though not half so dead as I would have liked to have rendered Jackson Abercrombie. An hour later the rotten man himself rang up, and I don't suppose I need to say how glad I was, what pleasure I felt, when this dreadful monster cancelled his visit.

HOW THE WHITE MOON GOD BECAME

In spite of our belief that we today originated them, the ancients appear to have been fully conversant in the techniques of genetic engineering. The story is told, for example (Genesis 30), of how Jacob tricked his uncle Laban out of his entire flock of sheep, by agreeing to divide the flock between the two of them, the white sheep going to Laban, the speckled to Jacob. Having struck this bargain, Jacob systematically bred out all the white sheep, leaving himself in sole possession of what was, by then, a most substantial flock.

Given that this is clearly intended less as a moral parable of trickery connivance and skulduggery than as an example of an aetiological myth, can we find any evidence of aetiological mythology behind other forms of genetic modification? How, for example, did the white moon-god, known in Hebrew as Ha Lavan, become transformed into the merely patriarchal uncle Laban? How did the woolly mammoth become the oryx, or the oryx the domesticated cow (the poet laureate Ted Hughes has made some interesting speculations on this subject)? Similarly the alpaca's reduction to mere sheepery, the crossing of the peach and plum to make the nectarine, the development of the pink grapefruit, the water-leaning tendencies of the white narcissus. Can we deduce a hesitancy to eat the killer of Adonis in the persisting taboo on pork? Is it ascertainable in what way the gods participated in the reduction of plantain to banana? And what of the domesticated cucumber, the tamed tomato, the housebound poodle or the cat curled up across the rug? Whatever happened to the wild, untrammelled, prickly rosacea that we transmuted into pot-plant? What heir of Pegasus or Bucephalus or Incitata will scurry over Beecher's Brook this April or attempt the Preakness? How did the Italian sonnet with its three conceits and single rhyme become transfigured into that picayune affair the Elizabethan, with its paltry two conceits and its easy double rhyme? And which came first, the butterfly or the caterpillar?

We have, of course, the tale of Frankenstein to teach us, albeit less genetic modification than anatomical reconstitution, complete with unfiled bolts. But what of the deliberate bisecting of eggs within the womb - a practice allegedly carried out throughout the middle ages by Jews and gypsies eager to blaspheme against the Christian God by generating twins (a most primitive form of cloning it's true, but cloning nonetheless)? What of the tampering with soil by means of fertilisers and re-agents, to force lettuces to change colour or to grow faster, to make white hydrangeas pink or green or blue? What of the forced modification of the genetic structure of the human mind by compulsory education?

You who sound the tocsins against genetic modification do not even know the toxins you are already poisoned with. The very ink with which you write your diatribes (and are not you, yourselves, the genetic modification of the algae into fishes, of the fishes into primates, of the primates into men?) was once the stomach juices of a sea-snail, crushed and mixed with sediment of rat. The very paper on which you publish your homilies was previously tree-trunk, whose sap was interspersed with excrement of pigeon. The very soft boiled egg you eat at breakfast while you read the published versions of your admonitions, why that egg was taken from a guinea-hen that had been cross-bred with a shilling-fowl (and much profit from the minting), and whose crushed bone-meal fed the flowers that you gave your wife last evening.

FOR LAWRENCE DURRELL

In Quinx, the final fragment of his "Avignon Quintet", the much underrated poet and novelist Lawrence Durrell posits a number of tales which he deems to be the "great themes" of the present world. Durrell posits, but doesn't actually write. I propose therefore to guess at how he might have chosen to complete them. They are set out as follows:-

✠   What did they think, the women who watched the Crucifixion?

☯   Buddha's wife became his first initiate, as did the daughter of Pythagoras.

♉   The one Spartan to outlive Thermopylae was left for dead on the field and came to himself when the enemy had gone. But he couldn't stand the odium of having escaped the slaughter, the suspicion of having run away. He killed himself in despair.

♋   A Don Juan who was terrified of women.

♋   Crusoe seen through the eyes of Friday.

These, then, are the premises. I will, shortly, venture to recount the tales. But first it might amuse the reader to learn this tale, drawn from Durrell himself:-

ON THE BRIDGE

Someone once said that heroism is merely cowardice, running in the wrong direction.

At the time when the Nazis occupied ancient Avignon, a vast cache of arms was delivered by railway from amongst the caverns and corridors of the Roman quarries of nearby Vers where it had been stored. The Nazis placed the train filled with this ammunition on the bridge over the Rhône at Avignon, in the dead centre of the town, and ordered the Austrian sappers who were in charge of it to blow up the train.

In an army in which the obeying of orders was regarded as both a religious duty and a self-vindicating act, the sappers did a most remarkable thing - they refused. Indeed, they mutinied rather than perform the deed, for to blow up the train would have caused not only the destruction of Avignon's bridge and the end for all time of dancing *tout en rond*, but of much of the mediaeval town as well. By their action the town was saved.

What followed is what makes the tale worth telling. The sappers might have been awarded medals for their heroism, or they might have been shot for mutiny and insubordination. In the event, they received both. As rebels, they were stood up against a wall, where they received the just reward of traitors. Yet no attempt was made to mock their action, nor to declare it futile, through the co-option of another team of willing dynamiters. The roses still placed annually by the townsfolk on the graves of the dead sappers, testify that they also received the just reward of heroes.

THE TWO MARIES

They had followed him, almost from the very beginning, Mary the wife of Zebedee and mother of his apostles James and John, and Mary from Migdal, the watchtower of General Tiberius by the Sea of Galilee. They had followed him when the city of Tiberius began to rise up stone by stone, driving the Zealot army into the hills. They had followed him when Shammai, the greatest Rabbi of their day, succumbed to old age and was succeeded by Joseph bar Kayafah, the man they called "the Rock". They had followed him to Cana and Beit Anatot and Genasseret, to Kfar Nachum and Tabgha, to all the places where he preached and stirred up controversy, announcing himself at these, the end of days. They had followed him despite the laughter, the mockery, the accusations of heresy, the vilifications of the Rabbis who had no better answer to the sins of men and the anger of God and the Roman occupation than to sit in Rabbi Joshua's garden by the Sea of Galilee and keep an egotistic record of their pointless arguments and commentaries. They had followed him as he proved to the people who he was by fulfilling each and every one of the prophetic auguries - the date palms and the donkey, the journey west from Bosrah, the desolation of the wilderness, the suffering, the denial especially. They had followed him, because he was who he was, and soon the swords would be turned into ploughshares, and the lion would lie down with the lamb.

They had followed him, too, south to the capital, lost at the back of an immense crowd, uncertain of events because Jerusalem was rife with rumour, but it appeared he had gone into the Temple as he had said he would, to bring about both its and his destruction, so that the Kingdom of God might come at last. He had been arrested, they heard, and praised the noble Judas for his valour. He had been sent to the High Priest Bar Kayafah, to the Roman Governor Pilate, had received the condemnation he expected, and now, this very eve of Passover, as the Angel of Death had passed over Egypt a thousand years before, so again this very afternoon the Hand of God would strike, the Arm of God would be outstretched, and Mankind would be liberated. Such sweet anticipation! Such hope! Such joy!

On the Hill of Calvary the Roman soldiers mocked and jeered the Azazel, and with their spears held back the crowds. But he was magnificent, the Suffering Servant incarnate, just as he had told them - his clothes torn from torturing, his hair wet with his own blood, his face the face of Isaac when he too climbed this hill of Moriah from which the Maries took their name, bearing the wood for his own sacrifice, longer ago even than the slavery in Egypt. "How long?" the Prophet Isaiah had asked. And now they knew. Until precisely now.

And then he turned to them.

"Daughters of Jerusalem, weep not for me, but for yourselves, and for your children. Behold, the days are coming in which they will say, 'Blessed are the barren, and the wombs which never bore, and the breasts that never suckled'. Then shall they begin to say to the mountains, 'Fall on us', and to the hills, 'Cover us'. For if they do these things in a green tree, what shall be done in a dry?"

It was completely unintelligible, but it didn't matter. No doubt he was quoting scripture. Or perhaps the Romans had deliberately drugged him. It didn't matter. Never in all of human history had any man looked quite this handsome, quite so - there really was no other word for it than "god-like". For all his stumbling under the weight of that Cross, for all the Roman jibes, the Jewish taunts, the dry heat of the April sun, the exhaustion visible in his features, the sound of nails hammering bone to wood. He was magnificent. He was - everything his followers had always known he would be, now, at this hour of his death, at the end of days, at the time predicted by the Prophets, at this instant of completion. Such sweet anticipation! Such hope! Such joy!

THE DISCIPLE

I found him where I had been told he would be found, seated under the bodhi tree at Kusinagra, surrounded by so many acolytes they darkened the space about him and proved his every teaching by the miserable noise and stench and clamour with which they prevented him from entering Nirvana. Yet he himself appeared not to notice them, not to be aware of hands grasping at his cloak, superstitious to touch some numen they imagined it to radiate, not to be aware of questions that he couldn't answer anyway, not to be aware even of my presence, grand-daughter of the Sakya Rajah of Kapilavastu, daughter of the Sakya Muni Siddhartha Gautama, not to be aware of the cicadas or the lotus leaves, not to be aware of poverty or undernourishment, not to be aware of light or smell. He appeared not to notice any of this, but all appearance is of course illusion, and he, the Buddha, was indeed aware.

I had come to seek my father, but I had failed to find him. I had come to seek my father, but I had found, instead, my path, my way, my goal. As to my father, it was evident that he had long ago traversed reality and entered the fruitful realm beyond. And as the realisation struck me, he looked into me, and said:

"My daughter, the Unreal never is, the Real never is not."

But the voice was my own voice, the insight my own insight, and the wind blowing through the curtains of the palace at Kapilavastu brushed the edges of the paper on which the bodhi tree was drawn, so that its leaves appeared to shimmer, and the eyes of the Buddha opened on eternity.

THE SPARTAN

"And I alone am escaped to tell the tale"
Herman Melville, *"Moby-Dick"*

Anyone who knows me might expect me to make of this the story of my father-in-law (who I never knew), who after months of argument and bribery and insult managed finally to leave Berlin for Australia, only days before the catastrophic Kristallnacht in November 1938 - he was just fourteen at the time - who settled in England as a doctor in the 1950s, but who never came to terms with the fate of his fellow Jews, and like his mother and grandfather and several uncles before him, took his own life at the third attempt in 1961 (significantly he gassed himself and left a note requesting cremation); it so obviously concurs with Durrell's intention, but still I shall not tell it (the tale of a lone survivor should only be told by that survivor, or at the very least a blood-relation, not a divorced in-law), even though, of course, in writing just this paragraph, I have.

DON JUAN

It was certainly true what people said of him, that he gazed yearningly and adoringly at every female, that you could literally watch the blinking of his eyes as mentally he undressed each one of them, as he imagined every physical sensation and every carnal act, as he pursued them, as he altered the routines of his daily life for them, as he gave up whole evenings to accompany them to restaurants and cinemas. Never actually *with* them, mind you. Rather, at what might be termed a safe, a reticent distance. Never quite able to bring himself to speak to them, let alone to carry out the elementary seductions which his imagination had conceived.

His studies of the female form were such as almost to constitute a science in themselves. He had worked out, for example, after many years of silent, solitary research on the beaches of Torquay and Morecambe, that the beauty of the female was in fact diminished and not enhanced, as might have been expected, with each layer of clothing that was taken off, and that this was especially true of those women who preferred their bathing topless - an activity he supported salivatorily in theory but was inevitably disappointed by in practice. He had also noted, and was in process of developing a mathematical formula something along the lines of Pythagoras' clichéd formulation, that hot weather arouses sexual desire in the male in precisely the same proportion that it reduces the capacity to fulfil it - the sunlight inducing women to remove layers of clothing, on the one hand, but draining all expendable energy from the male libido on the other.

Nevertheless his admiration knew no bounds. No bounds at all - which was precisely why the police at last arrested him. For he had begun to conduct his formal researches through the wrong end of a microscope, pointed at the unclosed curtains of many a suburban bedroom. For he had begun to satisfy his aesthetic theories in the contemplation of rather more video tapes and magazines than might have been considered normal for a normal adult male. For he had taken to pursuing the loveliest of women, not simply to cafés and theatres, but to their homes, their workplaces, even to the offices of their lawyers when they found just cause to protest against his ardour. For he had acquired the habit of writing letters to his loves, in prose befitting Abelard and poetry worthy of John Donne, and posting them by hand through letter boxes.

Yet what pleasure more innocent, more natural, more healthy, than a male in pursuit of Aphrodite? What crime less sinful than the sin of total shyness? What figure more quixotic, more pathetic, than the passionate Don Juan who dies by his own hand, tied by the throat to a beam in a police cell, still a virgin at forty-four?

MAN FRIDAY

Until he came, this island was a Paradise. The gods of our ancestors lived with us in peace, among the palm fronds and beside the surfless sea, and taught us the art of navigation and the craft of building ships with double hulls, rigged with claw-shaped sails and steered by dagger-board, so that none of us would have been so foolish as he was, who set sail upon the ocean in a craft that could capsize.

To build his shelter, he tore out roots of ancient trees and cleared a sacred grove. For food he gobbled down the fruit undried, so his terrible ablutions became a still more terrible pollution. His feet trampled the songlines, till their very staves were crushed. The stones he took to build his compound deprived us of the sacred memory of our ancestors.

I was sent ostensibly to serve him, because serving was deemed the safest way of monitoring his acts and limiting their damage. If I pretended to accept his ways, his gods, his gifts, this was only in deference and expediency. The truth was, I deplored the man, and would gladly have stabbed him in his sleep had this not been explicitly forbidden.

He liked, I know, to think of me as ignorant, and of himself as practically a god, and this I humoured, both by pretending to be the ape he thought I was, and by never humiliating him when he revealed his flaws. Yet without my aid, he would not have survived a fortnight. He called himself intelligent, cultured, civilised. But he could not hunt, nor cook, nor make clothing, nor build a shelter, nor see the traces of the other men and women who inhabited this island in their hundreds, not even the faces of the little children who watched him furtively from every secret cave and treetop; nor could he give an explanation for the rains not coming when he needed them, and this despite his daily prayers, nor for the failure of his friends to rescue him, despite the fire on the hilltop that would have used up every tree the island had if rescuers had not at last appeared by accident.

Now, at last, he has gone, and we are gladly rid of him. Yet the reliques of his presence still remain with us, and these will never go. Where he built his fire, the earth will not grow back. Where his false god walked, ours cannot set foot. The herds he killed for food are so diminished that the balance of nature is unsettled. Even to this day, our children still fall sick and die of his diseases.

THE UNIVERSAL LANGUAGE

"To be is to to do" - Spinoza
"To do is to be" - Sartre
"Do be do be do" - Sinatra

The aim (and surely no one will contest its worthiness) was not to create a universal language *per se*, but to find the ultimate and universal truth - a concept known as *hypostasis* - and with it to construct a universally perfect society. However, as the previous sentence more than adequately elucidates, this goal required precise language for its realisation, and so a universal language, a Babel-language, had to be created first.

The aims were threefold:

a)   universalisation

b)   simplification

c)   (and here there was, still is, a continuing dispute between the philosophers and the philologists, the former of whom argue that philosophers are by definition also philologists, the latter that philology is actually a variant and more accurate term for philosophy and that consequently the two disciplines are really one and the same [but that the two points of disagreement stated here are not]...the actual dispute in question being, not this semantic and ontological one, but whether the purpose of the form of the new language was to eliminate the human ego altogether [how else can society be perfected?], or simply to transfer the emphasis of language from one that is pronoun-based to one that is action-biased [as stated in a parenthesis on the final report: "{for example, in the sentence 'Mahmoud ointed a norange', the significance lies not in Mahmoud, nor even in the norange, but in the act of ointing, for it is action that justifies and validates the universe}]).

To give one example of simplification, it was agreed that the Arabic system of root-words should be adopted, allowing each root to be developed into verbs, nouns, participles, gerunds etc of interrelated meaning. Thus, in place of complex and incongruous terms such as "*to* write" but "*a* book", there is now the verb "to write" and the noun "a writing". This case is obvious and straightforward, where "a norange" and "to norange" are less obviously so. This latter case has, nevertheless, been cited as one of the supreme achievements of Bavel-*sprach* (the new universal language has thus far reached no further than western Europe, where the Germanic form appears to have become adopted by default even if not by common preference [attempts to simplify spelling, incidentally, have alas not succeeded, owing to a controversy {or at the very least a contention} over whether to introduce a fonetic or a phonetik system.])

The brilliance of this example lies in its capacity to meet all three requirements. As universalisation, the change from "an orange" to "a norange" redeems the word from its Anglo-Saxon colonialism and returns it to its Hispano-Latin root, "naranja"; similarly with "disorient", which has been recovered (or reoccidentated) from the solecism "disorientate" (a reverse example of this is "an anointment", which might have been reoccidented from the erroneous "an ointment", but has in fact been left in its simplified form, with the verb "to oint" – to the may of some and the dismay of others - created to support it. [The verb "to make love" has, by contrast, been eradicated altogether, on the grounds that, sadly, it is so rarely accurate.] As simplification it removes the confusion as to the exact process by which a norange is consumed, since it is neither definitely eaten nor precisely drunk, but it is self-evidently noranged. As to the third category, the verb is principally passive, which is demonstrably the most perfect form of the active verb known at the present time or likely to be evinced in the future.

While on this subject of the active and the passive, it has been observed that a perfect society is one in which all possible actions have already taken place (hence in language the description of the past as the perfect tense), and where all that remains for human beings to do is to imitate and to repeat (indeed, the verb "to do" does not appear anywhere in the new dictionary, having been replaced by the far more accurate verb "to repeat"). On the other hand, as stated earlier, action is seen as the ultimate justifier of existence, and so it is hardly surprising that a mystical cult has begun to form, which believes that a certain future time will one day arise when human beings will be freed from this bondage to imitation, when stories will no longer be mere anagrams of other stories and lives of other lives, when individuals will once again be free "to do" in the most creative and fulfilling sense.

The builders of this system, looking beyond language towards the universal perfection of society itself, at last published (in a commendable eighty-four international languages and seventeen regional dialects), the parameters, so to speak, of their "Paradigm for Paradise" (I think it was Auden who advised against alliteration in prose [and rightly; in the sub-clauses of the universal language all forms and fashions of alliteration have in fact been outlawed]). Their recommendations contained a number of radical ideas, although I hesitate to use the term "radical" since it was proposed to outlaw that too in the coming era. Similar words, such as "progressive", "civilised", "cultured", "educated", "intelligent", "informed", and even "correct" were all likewise anathematised, because they were deemed to have lost their intrinsic meanings and to have become mere synonyms for that most egocentric of all conceits, which the etymologists construe as "happening to concur with the expressed opinions of any individual speaker".

Following the Platonic tradition of banishing anything which the Platonist cannot brook, TV and cinema have also been banned because they discourage thinking and imagining. Books are permitted, but only under licence and in specific circumstances (such as medical prescription or for those deemed to be pathologically incapable of inhabiting reality). In addition books may not be read but can only be written out longhand; all humans are required, on the other hand, to write a book of their own "as frequently as time permits" - a phrase of astonishing looseness and generality given the context.

Education is to be banned before the age of sixteen, on the grounds that it steals a child's innocence, and that no child is mentally ready to be taught, since they lack the maturity to be discriminating or discerning in seeing what is and what is not worth learning.

For the same reason, nobody will be allowed to vote before the age of twenty-five, nor to stand for public office before the age of thirty-five, and even then only after rigorous training. Work will be so far encouraged that there is to be no income tax, but spending taxes will increase in proportion to the vanity and unimportance of the purchase.

The final pages of "The Code", as it has been humorously nick-named, contain an extraordinary peroration that would be tantamount to a divine revelation had God not also been abolished. The authors note that a *hypostasis* - a single Truth which transcends all particular truths and thereby renders them valid - is in fact self-defeating, by the following logic. The statement "all *hypostases* are false", if all *hypostases* were indeed false, would therefore be a true statement, which it could not be, since all *hypostases* have just been proven to be false. If, on the other hand, the statement rather than the *hypostases* were false, then the statement could not be made, in which case its opposite would have to be true. From this comes the logical deduction that all *hypostases* must therefore be true, which, since "all *hypostases*" includes and renders truthful all other statements, implies that every statement in the world must thus be true, including the statement that all *hypostases* are false, which they patently are not.

Astoundingly (again I am tempted to use the word "radical"), as a result of this realisation, the creators of the universal language have voted to abolish scientific endeavour altogether, including both philosophy and philology, from the new order. The argument is staggering in its ingenuity. Since all scientific endeavour is based upon the construction of paradigms that pretend to explain the universe, or aspects of the universe, through generalisations, and since all paradigms and generalisations are self-evidently and intrinsically false (which includes, by definition, the statement that all paradigms and generalisations are self-evidently and intrinsically false), then there is no end result achievable from the practice of science, and it should therefore be ended, though it cannot be, because the abolition of scientific endeavour would itself be an end result of scientific endeavour. In its place, nonetheless, they recommend a return to metaphysics, a subject which has now reached such profound depths of wisdom that all men have become firmly reconciled to the inevitability of death and decomposition, and, indeed, regard it as the only worthwhile goal, purpose and pursuit in life. This total reconciliation is known as Futilitarianism, and the worship of futile pursuits has now replaced the worship of *hypostases* (such as Church, Justice, Truth, Society, etc) as the main outlet of human activity - sport especially, but also, of course, the attempt to create a universal language, to find the ultimate and universal *hypostasis*, and to construct a universally perfect society.

However, the abolition of science has led to a decline to zero in the number of people capable of formulating a universal language or constructing a perfect society, and consequently both endeavours have now regrettably been abandoned.

DAEDALUS

Over many years, aided by the goddess Athene and a workshop of apprentices, he had invented any number of gadgets and devices, many of which were morally and socially useful, all of which, alas, were utterly unpatentable. There was, for example, the automatic redistribution-of-wealth machine, a sealed collection-box into which those who preferred not to be encumbered by the carrying of small coin could place any that befell them. There was the flying machine - his own son had died in testing it - which allowed a man to soar as high as hubris or as low as the plathid ocean wearing nothing but wax and feathers. There was the iron saw that he invented by pouring molten metal over the skeleton of a fish. There was the system for harvesting hot air inside the roofs of over-heated parliaments and council chambers, and storing it to give out as charity to old people in the winter. There was the potter's wheel, and the compass for marking out circles, and the machine that told jokes without ruining the endings, and of course the labyrinth. There was...there were many, many such contrivances.

After his escape from Crete (he had murdered his apprentice Talos out of jealousy and buried Icarus his son and feared his own judicial murder) he had the idea of inventing a machine that ran on suffering, with which he would be able to tap all the pain and misery in the world and harness it for the purpose of generating happiness. To patent and develop such an engine, however, required the support of venture capitalists, but none was willing to take it up, because the energy source would be self-destroying, and built-in obsolescence is only meaningful if a replacement can be sold.

MADONNA AND CHILD

My lady wanted to have a child, because this was one of her potentials and she liked to explore all of her potentials. I helped of course, in so far as a man can help in these matters. I participated in the conception of the thing. I looked after her. I suffered in sympathy. And sometimes, because I was jealous I suppose, I would have liked to have had a child myself, though this was absurd.

Then, when the child was born, I primed a canvas and painted a portrait of my lady with her child. It wasn't the same, of course. It was a creative act, but at a distance. It was Art, not Life.

That was three years ago. Now my lady talks about "our" child and "our" painting, but I know she's only humouring me. She says that women are slaves, but I can't agree with her. She doesn't have a slave mentality. It's I who has the slave mentality.

Now I would like to kill the child, because it has served the purpose for which it was created, and because it has dislodged the balance between my lady and myself. I could never actually kill it though. This afternoon I completed and then destroyed my fourteenth portrait.

THE CELL

Yesterday we could have made the revolution. We sat together talking about what we'd seen and what we'd learned, how the poor were starving and had no clothes, how the soil was barren and the women treated like mere chattels, how there was no work and no money, and somebody made a joke about how even the beggars would soon be bankrupt; and as we talked we knew we could have made the revolution there and then, because we also knew that, despite the poverty, we did possess one thing, and that was anger.

Today, however, the revolution seems a long way off. A man came from the Party to talk with us, and asked if we understood the nature of the things we know, such as why the poor were starving and had no clothes, and how come the soil was barren and the women treated like mere chattels, and who is it who decides to give out work and print the money, and somebody made a joke about how even the bankrupts would soon be beggars; and as we reasoned we began to understand the system, and our place in it, and who exactly we were fighting, and what for, and how a revolution needed careful planning, and waiting for the right moment, and then we also knew that, despite the poverty, we do possess one thing, and that is ideology.

INTERNET CAFE

Unlike those Internet cafés that exist beyond cyberspace, in what pre-computer-age folk still call reality (or even "real reality", dismissing ours as "merely virtual"), the Internet café I am hoping to establish is not some overpriced physical location at the junction of two worlds – or even, as Starbucks likes to claim, at the junction of every two streets - where people can carry out normal café pursuits while also playing on a lap-top. This café will exist exclusively in that ultimate realm of the human imagination which post-Luddite man has named the Internet (in ancient times it was known as Literature), and I am afraid you will therefore have to overpercolate your own coffee and spill your own cigarette ash in the sugar (I recommend the Turkish coffee mentioned by Pepys in Volume 3 of the Diaries; a good Virginian tobacco such as the one Sitting Bull is depicted smoking in Dugarry's portrait; and for the sugar, that you refer to the account of the cutting of the cane by negro slaves in William Faulkner's "The Four-Inched Bridge" - I would quote the words myself, but can't, for sadly these are all inventions.)

Thus far I have built the site but not yet created the menu, and to this end I invite my reader's interactive participation (what else is good literature, after all, but a two-way process, not of communication, but of mutual imagining?).

Because this café inhabits the virtual reality of literature, the menu must be taken exclusively from famous works of art and letters. Apples by Cézanne, of course. Inevitably tea must be served with madeleines. Leopold Bloom's breakfast is only available on June 16th. For contemporary litterateurs, there is an exquisite if excruciating Cantonese snakefeast in Colin Thubron's "Behind The Wall", and a number of Greek binges occupy the characters in Louis de Bernières account of "Captain Corelli's Mandolin". For the classicists of Eng. Lit., Dickens provides the full turkey beano in "A Christmas Carol", while elsewhere Sir Walter Scott elucidates two parallel menus, the Saxon of the farmyard and the Norman of the table, in which pig becomes pork, cow veal, bull beef and mutton a delicious casserole laced with cider and rosemary. Others may like to assemble a more eucharistic pre-Easter dinner, based on whichever Last Suppers and the details of the seder plate complete with blood of Christian baby. For dessert Caravaggio has some delicious fruit, and not only oranges.

I will publish (on the Internet, where else?) any menus of sufficiently high aesthetic standard that are sent to me - by e-mail, obviously: theargamanpress@yahoo.co.uk is the address.

And while waiting for the menu to arrive, a few ideas for further myths and parables, unwritten as yet by me, but which you might like to turn your hand to, and send to the above address - interactive stories, so to speak. As follows:

* a proof that, other than the English histories, the plays of Lord Southampton and Francis Bacon weren't written by them at all, but by an upstart Warwickshire farmer named William Shakespeare (or Shakespere or possibly Shakspear); and that his weren't authentic either, but simply translations from the Italian of a series of courtly comedies and romances in the *commedia dell'arte* tradition. The tale must include extracts from the original Italian folios (you will have to invent these), and a commentary illuminating the errors in the English versions.

* the notion that time is not some theoretical abstraction after all, but physical, physiological, a function of memory; told through the case of a total amnesiac who is obliged to live in a permanent state of present.

* a new version of - almost any great novel would do, but let's say "One Day In The Life Of Ivan Denisovitch" - in which the names of the characters are replaced by - almost any location would do, but let's say South Africa - Bantu and Afrikaans names, as are the names of places and, inevitably, the odd other word here or there, but where, in all other dimensions, the identical words are set out in the identical order to tell the identical tale.

* a story written in any language, but constructed in such a manner that it is literally untranslatable into any other.

* the autobiography of God, written unselfconsciously, without remorse.

* a modern reworking of the legend of Croesus, who was told by the Delphic oracle that he would be responsible for the destruction of an empire, without being told that the empire in question would be his own.

* openings for tales based on the openings of famous tales, but modified in the way that Rachmaninov composed his variations on a theme of Paganini. Borges has such an opening to "Utopia Of A Tired Man", which modifies "Anna Karenina" into "no two hills are alike but everywhere on earth plains are one and the same"; Gide has similarly modified the "Call me Ishmael" of "Moby-Dick" into the "Call me Nathaniel" of his "Nourritures Terrestres", and St John of Patmos the opening of the "Book of Genesis" in his "Revelation". The opening of "Orlando" by Virginia Woolf is too easy and may not be used.

* a life of Jesus out of Freud and vice versa.

* a "Tale of Tales" in the manner of Rabbi Nachman of Breslau, in which the first tale is left unfinished because a second tale sprouts out of it, and then from that a third, and so on, to infinity.

* the application of a man's theories mirroristically, against himself, to test both out. Thus, perhaps, a detailed psychoportrait of Sigmund Freud; a glossary of those terms stolen by Jung from the universal unconscious; a dialectical appraisal of Hegel; St Paul seen through a glass darkly; an essay on "mauvaise foi in the writings of Jean-Paul Sartre"; or on "failure to render thought into being in the works of Rene Descartes"; a discussion of whether Leibnitz was the best of all possible philosophers; a proof of the authority of Newton over Galileo by throwing a copy of "Principia Mathematica" over the side of the leaning tower of Pisa; the theories of Kepler through the wrong end of a telescope; the relative values of Einstein et al...

* a series of mnemonics, in verse form, for the purpose of remembering mnemonics (or even of remembering what mnemonics are).

* a list of books, not including the obvious examples such as commonplace books, books of aphorisms, quotations and proverbs, or collections of compressed and minimal short stories, which are best read last-page-first and then presecutively to the beginning.

* the (whimsical?) tale of a man who spends a night in a haunted house, but nothing untoward occurs because these are sceptical ghosts who do not believe in human beings.

A SINGULAR JUDICIAL PROCEDURE

Today is July 22nd 1916, the day on which Joseph K is stabbed to death in his prison cell, an event recorded in all its unique peculiarity in the diary of his brother Franz, the namesake of the great Czech novelist. The condemned man (we are not told for what he has been condemned) is stabbed to death in his cell by the legal executioner (convention asks us to imagine a tall, heavily-built man, a kind of mediaeval yeoman with a black mask and a woodchopper's axe; whereas on this occasion it's actually a bespectacled grey figure in a clean, dark suit, a civil servant who failed his medical training and likes to golf on Sundays, the sort who waters his flowers and his car each evening, in the hope that both will grow), without any other person permitted to be present. How exactly does it happen?

Joseph K is seated at the table (the only furniture, besides his cot, that is permitted), finishing yet another of those interminable letters of self-vindication to his father; or perhaps the last plate he will ever savour of his favourite *kugel* pudding. A rattle of locks is heard, unambiguous and yet indifferent; it's the executioner.

"Are you ready?" he asks.

The content and sequence of his questions and actions are precisely fixed for him by regulation; he may not depart from this. It's a doubly necessary process. It raises the event to the status of a ritual, a ceremony, a sacred rite, akin to Temple sacrifice. It removes the burden of humanity from the executioner, rendering him a priest of justice, excusing him from personal guilt.

The condemned man, who at first jumped up - fear induces mirages; he had momentarily mistaken the arrival of the executioner for that visit from his brother he had repeatedly requested - now sits down again and stares straight before him, or buries his face in his hands.

Having received no reply, the executioner opens his instrument case on the cot, chooses the silver daggers with the inlaid mother-of-pearl handles, and, not meaning to upset Joseph K but simply to ensure the cleanness of the operation, he tests and sharpens the edges of the blades. Darkness has set in by this time, actually as well as metaphorically. The executioner sets up a small lantern - a simple tallow candle in a glass and metal box - and lights it; but it's a stage lamp to spotlight a denouement, and not in any moral sense illuminatory. The condemned man furtively turns his head towards the executioner, shudders when he sees what he's doing, wonders momentarily whether the intention is the throat or ribs, then turns away again. This act of turning away is essential, to denote the evil of what is about to be enacted. But it also expresses a desire to see no more. Light, after all, is no longer pertinent.

"Ready," the executioner says after a little while.

And what surprises is the absence of a question-mark.

So much so, that Joseph K inserts his own.

"Ready?" he ejaculates, jumping up and now looking directly at the executioner. "You're not going to kill me," he says, and it's a statement made in absolute conviction. "You're not going to lay me down on that cot and simply stab me to death." Such a small and fragile man, he couldn't have managed it anyway, without the full cooperation of the victim. But it's no longer a statement of fact. Lack of a response has reduced it to a mere assertion of intention to resist. "You're a human being, after all." He seems now almost to be pleading. Certainly the hiatus in that last phrase was sufficient to deserve a comma. "You can execute someone on a scaffold, with assistants and in the presence of magistrates, but not here in this cell, one man killing another!"

But the executioner merely bends over his case, and does not answer.

"It's impossible," the man who was once Joseph K but is now only "the condemned man" adds more quietly.

And still the executioner says nothing.

"This singular judicial procedure" - Joseph K is trying to sound like his own lawyer, to give strength and credence to his hapless statements - "was instituted precisely because it's impossible to expedite. The form has to be preserved, but the death penalty is no longer carried out. You'll take me to another jail. I shall probably have to stay there a long time, but they won't execute me."

The moral certainties that have driven his whole life reside still in these statements - he is thinking, for example, of the ancient law of Moses which redeems the lamb that goes unwillingly to slaughter. But beyond the moral, he now sees that nothing in the world is ever certain.

The executioner now loosens a new dagger from its cotton sheath. The others, it transpires, were just frighteners after all. But this, this is the Abrahamic knife, the one prepared exclusively for Joseph K.

When suddenly, but calmly, unexpectedly, as if in dinner-party conversation, and yet stupendously, the executioner breaks his statutory silence. "You're probably thinking of those fairy tales," he says, "the ones in which a servant is commanded to expose a child, but out of cowardice or pity he doesn't do so, instead he binds him over as apprentice to a shoemaker. But those are fairy tales. This, this..."

He interrupts his own sentence, because this is not the sentence he has come into the cell to end. Yet Joseph K is reassured, returned to certainty by the very words the executioner has used, the very fact of speaking. This act of judicial murder is a legal ritual, governed by precise rules. By speaking outside the script (unless, perhaps, this too was scripted), by introducing this human moment, the executioner has created grounds and circumstances for a technical appeal. Even without witnesses, he knows that he is legally now saved, spared, redeemed by the human moment. Joseph K stands indomitable in the darkness of his cell, away from the cot and the spent lantern, waiting for the plunging of the knife. He cannot know if it will kill, or be withdrawn in unexpected clemency. But it matters not a jot. Joseph K is utterly content. In all this world, nothing is rarer nor more satisfying than the certitude, absolute and unequivocal, of being in the right. So he raises his arms, preparing to resist. So he begins to wrestle with what is not an angel, but a man, of death.

DOPPELGANGER

Gazing at the wonderfully porcelain features of Van Dyck's "Viola de Gamba Player" at the Alte Pinakothek in Munich (I have never been there; a friend showed me a photograph), and seeming to recognise in those features - the eyes especially, that stare out sideways like the personification of *vanitas* - a brilliant former student of mine, now safely ensconced amid the ivory towers and dreaming spires of Oxford, I found myself rehearsing an idea for a story, one which picked up a tendency that's almost a leitmotif in W.G. Sebald's "Vertigo", and which is also hinted at (I wonder if Sebald knew this?) in Herzog's meeting with his childhood friend Nachman in Saul Bellow's novel of that name. Still in rehearsal, it runs something like this:

A man keeps seeing people who resemble the famous dead, recognising them from photographs or portraits, aware that neither of these forms is ever entirely accurate, for they freeze a single instant of a face's life, whereas actual faces are ephemeral and transitory. He undertakes two strands of research, on the one hand trying to find out more about the resembled, on the other about the resembler, and on every occasion he discovers deep but impossible concordances. (My student, for example, hails from Windsor, where Van Dyck stayed during his visit to England in 1620; he died at his studio in Blackfriars, in a building that no longer exists, but where a modern bank now stands, in which my former student's brother is employed).

To research the resembler requires friendship, and the stories of these friendships become part of the narrative of the research. An entire trans-historical novel can thus develop, in which the narrator's own life becomes inextricably bound up in that of the historic figure, whom he can no longer distinguish from the doppelganger ("had supper with Cicero last night; he showed me the letter he was about to send to Caesar and I advised him to amend it"..."Buonarotti turned up unexpectedly for dinner with his new boyfriend"..."I have written to the papers about this incident in Würms; how can the world stand by and simply do nothing?"...) The scope for such a book is as infinite as history and the human imagination themselves.

For anyone wishing to develop this idea (I shan't do so myself; it's immense as an idea, but truthfully not worth the trouble of three hundred pages), I would urge avoiding the obvious trap of making the doppelganger conceit itself the central focus of the book; far better to feed it as a leitmotif, allowing it to crop up intermittently and incidentally as a sub-theme of a bigger novel. (For anyone wishing to develop this idea, which as I say I do not intend to do myself, the idea, and therefore the rights to the idea, remain nevertheless my own, and royalties will be expected.)

There are, of course, alternate routes into such a story, though perhaps they're not as interesting. Instead of befriending the lookalikes, the narrator may prefer to stalk and murder them - this would make the novel more filmable, and therefore more readily commercial in the American market. Or, instead of meeting the modern re-embodiments in real locations, he may discover them too in photographs and paintings (there's a figure in Picasso's "Guernica", for example, who is quite uncannily reminiscent of a certain Raphael "Madonna"; and a Jane Bown photograph of David - now Lord - Owen, some years ago in "The Observer", suggested precisely the ghoulish, white-faced figure whom Bram Stoker had in mind). Or perhaps the doppelganger can be encountered vice-versa - obsessed by the faces of certain trans-historical characters, the narrator seeks them out and convinces himself he's found them, even in the most unmatchable of doubles. Whichever way, what all this describes is merely a man who cannot or will not distinguish art from reality, who believes his affection is reciprocated by the authors and artists he admires, who cannot understand why the resemblers reject his approaches, unwilling to be the doppelgangers of the famous, anxious only to assert their own identities[3].

In my version of the novel, were I to write it, the characters would be the reality, and their actual lives would echo the previous lives of those whom they resemble - an unexplored conjunction of Nietzsche with H.G. Wells. Thus "The Clerk Macbeth" earlier in this collection. Thus Buonarotti as a waiter at the calabash restaurant on Greek Street who happens to be called Spiro Spiromades.

What might be best of all is not to write the book, nor even the idea, at all, but a fake review of the imaginary novel, and then create another doppelganger as the author to whom it is attributed...

---

[3] *For some reason the doppelgangers of Elvis Presley are an exception to this rule.*

THE ATLAS

When I was thirteen, amongst the gold cuff-links, the Gary Player golf clubs, the Swiss wrist watches, the silver Schaeffer fountain pens, and all the other expensive material objects whose acquisition seems to be the main purpose of the modern *Bar Mitzvah*, I received - I think it was my Uncle Martin in Australia who sent it - a magnificent world atlas, complete not only with maps of every land mass, but of the oceans too, and even a few photographs and diagrams of that one infinitude that can outdistance the minds of Man and God, by which I mean the Universe itself.

For years that followed I read and read, learning to decipher those complex codes of hill and vale, plain and river, learning to distinguish between the many shades of green and brown and blue that denoted wood rather than forest, sand rather than scrub desert, lake rather than reservoir. I learned the magical or comical names of towns - Potlogi in Romania, for instance, or Jammalamadugu in Andhra Pradesh, or that obscure village in south-west Poland which gave my own family its name, or the reality of Timbuktu, which turned out genuinely to exist, in Mali should you wish to check. I learned how geography was imposed as politics in Africa, as language in South America, as religion in the Middle East. I discovered that the temperament of islanders is different from that of people who inhabit archipelagos, and different again from mainlanders; but that even mainlanders vary as much by the size of that mainland, the number of its rivers, the height of its mountains, and even the propensity of its landscape to produce wine or beer or spirits.

Like Drake and Cook and Columbus and Magellan, I circumnavigated the globe repeatedly, sailing in a ship of maps, powered by the wind of my imagination. My journeys were both the same and very different from the voyages of Darwin; what I brought back was commensurate with though not identical to the discoveries of Raleigh. Each of us, after all, reads the waves (I'm thinking as I say this of Italo Calvino's Señor Palomar, of Jann Martel's Pi, of Virginia Woolf's poetic novel, of Coleridge of course, and Melville and Jonah) in his own way. Each of us learns by his own experience that the sea (I could say the same of the desert, the pampas, the ice-cap, the fjord) is never constantly nor singularly nor uniformly blue, but a shifting amalgam of colours defined by light and depth - turquoise flowing into cobalt, aquamarine merging into sapphire - white in the boat's wake, in some places as translucent as a mirage of water in the tarmac of a summer road, in others a pure white, luminously incandescent, where the sun spotlights it through clouds.

In all the years that passed, I continued to make these fabulous journeys, until I had visited every village, every jungle, every scree and every bourne, until I had explored every known and unknown region of the Earth. Better this, I came to understand, than any journey in the real world. No risk of shark or scurvy for my crew; no fear of mutiny if I asked them to round the Tierra del Fuego in a storm or to seek the north-west passage. No danger from those aborigines who ended the vain dreams of Ludwig Leichardt somewhere in the region of Ayers' Rock. No three-hour waits at airports, and then the constant fear of hijackers or deep-vein thrombosis. And better still, for there were journeys I could make which they, the earthbound pilgrims, could not, visiting those obscure antarctica where neither road nor rail nor plane had yet found access, crossing those borders which kings and potentates denied, fording rivers otherwise impassable for flood, tunnelling beneath mountains whose granite would prevent them.

So many hours have I spent, poring over my marvellous book of dreams, that year by year its pages have become damaged, its spine dishevelled, whole states wiped out by coffee stain, whole human habitations torn up by the interventions of a clawing cat. Now, finally, the universe has disintegrated altogether, and like some interplanetary deity dumping blueprints from the first draft of Creation, I have been forced to dustbin what is anyway the useless and anachronistic model of a world moved on. My wife has offered to purchase a new atlas, but I have declined. I know the world of this new volume will not be the one with which I am familiar (not only names of lands have changed, but borders have shifted, volcanoes have erupted, seas have dried up, whole rainforests have been transformed into polystyrene boxes for the taking home of hamburgers). Instead I have agreed, for the first time ever and with considerable reluctance, that we will undertake a journey in the real world, a physical adventure, to celebrate our grandson's *Bar Mitzvah* at that point marked 31.47 north by 35.13 east which I am told is called the Western Wall, and then a fortnight 2.16 degrees south of there, on the Red Sea at Eilat. This, at my age - too old now to explore another universe - will suit me far better than the revised atlas, which unlike reality can only engender disappointment.

THE BIG EVENT

Announcements had been appearing in the press for several weeks. The Big Event, they declared. The most momentous happening in the city for a hundred years. Be There.

Two-word, three-word proclamations. Just a slogan, a logo, no detail. You had to wait for several weeks and put the ads together like a jigsaw puzzle, even to begin to get the flavour of it. Capital Park. Sunday June 21st. Be There. People said it was the Second Coming, and they may have meant Jesus Christ or the Rolling Stones for all you knew. People said Politics. Sport. Religion. The Big Con. You began to hear that more and more. I'm not going. Nobody that I know is. Capital Park. Be late and you'll miss it. Entrance £15.00. That only appeared in the second week of June, by which time everyone had decided one way or the other. If you'd made arrangements to go, well £15.00 was next to nothing and you expect to pay. And if you weren't going anyway…

More than 200,000 people turned up at Capital Park that day. It was one of those events that everybody knew they couldn't miss. Even those who had sworn they wouldn't go, not even if they heard it really was the Messiah and the judgement of their souls depended on it. Everyone was there. It was one of those events you knew before it happened you would tell your grandchildren.

"So what happened, granddad?"

"300,000 of us turned up. You couldn't move for people. It was incredible."

Even the precise exaggeration was a necessary aspect of the telling.

"Yeah, but what happened?"

"What happened? Nothing? Nothing happened. It was a big con. Someone was trying to make fools of us and they succeeded."

And your grandchildren thought, that's right, they made total idiots of you. But wished there could be a big event like that in their lifetime as well, so they could say they wouldn't go, but go, so they could exaggerate the numbers, so they could have grandchildren who would go off thinking, 300,000 people at £15.00 a time, even after you count the cost of advertising, that's one hell of a big event in the world of con.

THE EDICT

Almanacs record that, on Monday August 21st, 1923, the city of Kalamazoo, in the American state of Michigan, passed a law prohibiting dancers from staring into their partner's eyes. Was this the consequence of some extraordinary scandal (I try to imagine some mid-western Lothario seducing the governor's daughter by optic mesmerism; and the ensuing scandal which prompted the legislature to act)? Was it simply a right-wing reactionary, or a morally-impelled Christian fear - these two are not always easily distinguishable - of the influence of such intense communication upon the virginally adolescent? Was it perhaps a by-product, an extension, of the prohibition of alcohol? Or was it something specific to the town, or to the name, of Kalamazoo, some Comanchee superstition, some Sioux ordinance, re-invoked in the cause of Amer-Indian reparations (how does a city get to be called Kalamazoo anyway, with or without people looking blushingly into each other's eyes?)? And how on earth do you police such a law, let alone provide suitable punishments for breaches? Was there perhaps an over-zealous misinterpretation here, of the biblical injunction to take an eye for an eye? And if so, where do the biblical teeth find their equivalent?

Are there - there surely must be - other instances of edicts of this kind? Once again I invite my readers to collaborate in a process of interactional creative writing, by supplying me (apologies; I mean, of course, by contributing) further specimens of such absurd and impracticable edicts, real preferably, though why not fictional (please also supply suggested punishments)? A few of the more obvious that come to mind are:

A law banning mothers from breast-feeding left-side before right.

A law forbidding the use of the index finger for pointing.

A law preventing black people from sitting on certain benches or attending certain schools.

A law prohibiting smiling on Thursdays (this may resolve my earlier question about the Biblical teeth).

A law requiring Jews to wear a yellow badge.

A law outlawing crass human stupidity.

A law banning poets from the Republic.

A law equating angles with hypotenuses, or mass and energy with light, or time with speed and distance, none of which could ever be enforced by humans.

A law, ineligible to repeal, absolutely and unequivocally precluding any form of dogma.

A law against satire.

A law against laws.

THE SURRENDER

If God is dead, then everything, as Dostoievski mooted in "The Brothers Karamazov", everything is permitted.

To Hiroo Onoda, God wasn't God but heroism, the Emperor, a nation's loyalty, the sword of the Samurai, and an individual's faith and honour; God was the rising sun, and nothing was permitted except that which the Emperor sanctioned by his own authority.

A man without a home, a wife, a family, a job, a salary, a car, a season ticket to the No plays or the baseball, a man without an ornamental garden, a copy of "The Pillow Book of Shei Shonagon" or the novelettes of Mishima, a man without a cherry tree, a jade vase or an incense stick, a man without a camera or a grey suit or a diploma in American English, may still live a full and happy life, even in the vast, empty hunger of the tropical rainforest, alone, abandoned and presumed dead; but a man without beliefs is less than a man, however trite or illusory or credulous those beliefs might be; such a man cannot endure.

Hiroo Onoda believed in the divinity of the Emperor, in the justice of the invasion of China, in the invincibility of his nation's forces on land and air and sea, in the demoniacal threat posed by the Yankees and the unbreakable promises of the Axis allies. He believed in the perfection of the Haiku and the Tenka, in the extension of the act of hara-kiri into the kamikaze martyrdom of Japanese air crews, in the significance of the tea ceremony, in the need to bind the feet of teenage geishas, in the famed cruelty of Filipino aboriginals, in the capacity of dead men to return in nightmare in order to seek vengeance on their murderers, in the preferability of black olives over green, in the linguistic inversion of Tokyo into Kyoto, in the virtues of acupuncture and the proven perspicacity of babies born on Sundays. By no means a gullible man, he believed in the solidity of the earth in the vicinity of his native Fuji, in the promises of the regional authorities that trains would run on time, in the aphrodisiacal properties of crushed ivory, in the assertion of the Royal Chamberlain that an heir would soon be born, in the military maps published in the newspapers which showed the great advances of the army into Indo-China, and in the probability that smoking cigarettes would lead to cancer.

As Yamanoue Okura had written of the fisher-folk of Shika in Chikuzen, more than twelve hundred years earlier, "Though not commanded by our Imperial Lord, by his own will Arao sailed, waving his sleeves as a sign that the sea was running high." So by his own will did Hiroo Onada join the Imperial army, and wave his soldier's sleeve as a sign that the triumphant tide of Japanese ascendancy was running high. So in the darkness of Lubang Island, in the archipelago of the Philippines, on March

10th 1974, 29 years after a bomb at Nagasaki had fractured the rising sun into a billion radioactive shards and all his fellow-countrymen save only he had abandoned the myths of loyalty and faith, so by his own will Hiroo Onoda accepted at last that God was dead, and that amongst that "everything" which was now permitted, there was included the ultimate dishonour of his personal surrender.

THE MODEL IN THE DESERT

In a vain attempt to prove that he was, not simply the gods' representative on Earth, but a god in his own right, the Pharaoh Aken-Tamun announced his intention to build a second copy of his kingdom, a replica complete with oceans, mountains, even moon and stars; and thereby to achieve the double aim of this demonstration of his divinity, and also the utilisation of the vast and pointless desert that occupied his empire's centre. The enterprise required several years, but there at last it was, the whole empire - or anyway a scale-model; but he was happy to accept this, just as he was happy to be acknowledged as himself only a scale-model of the actual divinity - every town, every love affair, every cactus, every prison, the sea stretching to that limited infinity which is the visible human horizon, even the moon and stars about which so many of his populace complained, for he had done no more than borrow the existing orbs and constellations, to re-deploy the primal sun. Yet the facsimile was in every way perfect - there were even those same species of grasshopper in the northern marshes that didn't exist in the southern hills, those same unique varieties of bougainvillea that so depended on the quality of lime within the soil that they couldn't subsist on any other; even the proportion of ants to armadillos had been precisely calculated. Perfect then, but still in vain. For it remained a facsimile. It remained an act of imitation, and of plagiarism. It remained, in short, less than, other than divine. It existed, not in the galactic spheres, but in a mere transformed desert. It added no original substance to the original substance of the universe, but merely copied. And in copying, it copied nothing that lay beyond the boundaries, whether of the imperial domains or that limited infinity which is the visible human horizon.

Records of the 18th dynasty in which the accounts of this enterprise are given, also note the destruction of the model in the desert, the suicide of the Pharaoh, a plague of grasshoppers that crossed into the southern fringes of the desert, feeding on the limestone deposits, and finally eradicating six unique varieties of bougainvillea that had previously adorned the hillsides and the coastal plain. It may have been these records, rather than the statue of the Sphinx at Thebes, which inspired the divine poet Shelley to pen his Ozymandias.

JUAN SAGLIERO

In his diary entry for July 26th 1894 - the birthday, incidentally, of Aldous Huxley, and one year later of Robert Graves; the deathdays, eight years apart, of Atahualpa and Francisco Pizarro - the memoirist Juan Sagliero proposed the genre "Retrospective Writing", claiming to have thought it up that very afternoon in a café on the Rio Plato; where the truth is that Juan Sagliero was one of several pseudonyms of the Lanarkshire poet John Sayle, that he had stolen the idea from his former university tutor's doctoral thesis, and that he was actually writing up his diary in a public house in Glasgow a century and three months later than the given date. Borges would have made a lovely story out of this conceit - and somewhere in the unpublished-in-English collected prose there must be one. I conjecture that it reads as follows:

"Juan Sagliero's life was an illusion, and should not be confused with his literary outpourings, though appearance would suggest that it was the literary outpourings which are the illusion, since they contain nothing but the long invention of his literary life, fabricated as a diary at the end of each dull day on which he had, in fact, polished the iron links of wage slavery as an insurance clerk..."

No, three faults. Borges would have chosen an English pseudonym, for precisely the same reason, but invented, that I have chosen a Spanish, and vice versa for the real name. Borges would never have used so heavy and slighting a phrase as "literary outpourings", as this risked rebounding in aspersions against his own good self. Thirdly, Borges would not have made his character an insurance clerk (a mistake I myself made with my "Clerk Macbeth"), lest this encourage future decoders of the literary hieroglyphic to read in the name of Kafka, thereby reducing to the individually specific a parable that was intended universally. Lastly, Borges would never have had the arrogance or lack of manners to impute so dogmatic a list to such a revered master, not even retrospectively. And finally, Borges would never have admitted three faults when he knew perfectly well he had made four, or, as it now transpires, five.

"Sagliero's account of his visit to Afghanistan, based entirely on his reading of Byron's 'Road to Oxiana' and Bruce Chatwin's various letters, is probably the most intimate and rewarding account of Pashtun life ever set to paper; while his annual holidays in St Tropez and St Paul de Vence – 'booze and bimbos last year, shagging and Chagall this' is one of many vulgarities that undermine what is otherwise an elegant and tasteful oeuvre - coinciding as they did with actual rain-swept fortnights on the artificial beach at Weston-Super-Mare, offer tangible evidence (if such is needed) that the human imagination is always far more vibrant than the human reality, and that (contrary to the common misconception) travel in the physical rather than the mental serves actually to narrow and not expand the mind…"

Borges' tale - which is a fractionally different tale in each of the languages into which it has been mistranslated - both describes and contains the notion that one can never actually compose in the present, even when one uses the present tense to engender that illusion. By necessity, to write is to reflect upon the past, however recent. So a diaristic account of the day gone by, even one that attempts to marshal real events and call their roll (even one as detailed as Joyce's diary of June 16th 1904), is as much "historical fiction" as are Juan Sagliero's febrile imaginings or James Savage's recounting of the life of Alcibiades (JS, as you may have guessed, is another of John Sayle's *noms-de-plume*).

So we should learn to mistrust all writing, to regard as fiction even that which passes itself off as fact (this is Juan Sagliero's contention in the "Retrospective Writing" diary entry; his complete diary entries further both evidence and proof). I, for example, am writing these lines in my own diary under Monday January 31st 2000, but am actually doing so on Sunday February 6th, catching up the blank pages from which the insurance office has kept me far too busy these past weeks, and putting into the tale an idea first scribbled in a notebook half a decade ago, in a café on the Rio Plato in Borges' version, in a pub in Glasgow in my mistranslation, suggested by a reading of the doctoral thesis of my tutor at…no, delete that last line, as Borges did, noting in his diary that he had added it "for the worst of reasons, literary effect".

ETYMOLOGIES

I have long been fascinated by etymologies, and especially by those words which come into a language entirely by accident[4]. That "ketchup" should be an anglicisation of the Indonesian "kao-choup", or a "bungalow" a failure to recognise the word "Bengali", are merely errors of pronunciation. Other errors transfer in the culture as well as with the language: brandy, for example, which was originally brandy-wine, from the Dutch *brandewijn,* or "burned wine", a practice fortunately not carried out in the Loire or the Champagne. As a child my sister and her friends liked to make me "apple pie beds", which involved turning over the undersheet so that I couldn't get in properly. "Apple pie" wasn't precise, however. In French a folded sheet is "une nappe pliée". I strongly suspect that Guy Fawkes was similarly a variant of Guy Faux, not a man at all but a straw effigy used throughout Europe for centuries, at All Hallows Eve, to burn away the last of the summer harvest and clean away the evil spirits before sewing next year's crop.

None of these though are the one I came here to recount. The Hebrew root *"pasas",* gleaned from the Chaldean, means "to spread" or "scatter", and is generally used to imply successful harvests, as in Psalm 72:16 "Let there be abundance of corn in the earth – *yehi pisat bar ba-aretz".* From this root came the common term *"pas",* meaning "a handful of corn", or simply a portion – for corn was the staple diet of the time – and that itself evolved to mean, specifically, a portion of bread, as in the *"Yehi Ratson"* prayer of *Minchah Yom Kippur: "Keshem she-natata pisat lechem le-echol –* just as you gave a portion of bread to eat".

A portion of bread in ancient Israel tended to be round, and flat, and baked in an open oven. The Greeks, who conquered Israel, acquired the habit of eating it in the same manner, but struggled to pronounce it properly, and made the "s" a "t" - pita. The Roman soldiers, when they conquered Israel, found the flatbread dry and tasteless, and so they added a slice of tomato, and melted cheese. Whether confused between the "s" and the "t", or simply because this is how Italian is spoken, their descendants changed the middle consonant to a much more exotic double-z.

---

[4] *Wikipedia, that much-maligned student resource which teachers fear only because it risks rendering them redundant, has an extensive list at the website*
http://en.wikipedia.org/wiki/Category:Lists_of_English_words_of_foreign_origin

GASPARD

Gaspard had reached the end of painting. That's to say, he had mastered every genre, every form, every technique of the painter's craft, but still he hadn't found any visual language articulate enough to express what he needed to express. Worse, decades of reviews and criticism, of eavesdropping on the conversations of those people who attended his exhibitions, had taught him that a painter paints in the language of paint, but that a spectator always and automatically paraphrases back into the language of words, in order to derive meaning from the painted object.

Why not, then, Gaspard decided, cut out the middleman and paint words directly? The second phase of his glittering career was initiated and can be summed up by that question - years of painting letters that looked like faces, love, houses, Madonnas with Child, trees, war, landscape, the passage of time, whiteness, death; or whole words that were indeed just words, standing alone or conjugated into sentences. Even without reading the vitriolic defamations of the critics, Gaspard knew that these works were failures, for it isn't possible to hang language in a gallery and call it Art.

Or perhaps it is? Perhaps there is a way, and perhaps Gaspard discovered it. His final exhibition, in Paris in the same year that he abandoned painting altogether in favour of the noble profession of tax-collector, consisted of a series – precisely 12, the apostolic, the tribal, the constellatory number – of white canvases, all of different sizes, all, if you looked closely enough, of slightly different shades of white, all painted with different materials, on different types of canvas. And underneath each one, in dull stencil, their titles: "The Emperor's New Clothes", "Black Canvas with Eraser Marks", "Snowstorm", "Homage à Wilkie Collins", "Apple Blossom", "Acid Dream", "Still Life", "White Canvas", "Ceci n'est pas une Pipe", "The Hole in a Henry Moore", "Polo Mint", "Self-Portrait".

Where the critics had acclaimed the first phase of his career, and universally derogated the second, opinion was entirely divided over the merits of these final works.

THE FUTURE

Thursday February 7th 2008

Every day, The New York Observer offers its readers a summary of history yet to be, advance warning on the day's planned events, as though history were safe ground for prediction. So, we are told, today, at 11am, the World Health organisation will report on global tobacco use and control efforts (with cigarette breaks every 30 minutes, but only if you go outside, stand 20 metres from the building, and recycle your biodegradable butts into the rose bushes). At the same time, if they can get there in the dense traffic, the Transportation Committee will hear future taxi plans, while immigrant advocates and hospital officials will announce an initiative to improve access to health care for non-English speakers, where, in the Beth Israel Hospital Board Room, когда? at 11 o'clock I told you already, donde?, deuxième étage, σας ευχαριστούμε. At 3pm, shortly after a failed assassination attempt on the President of South Timor, there will be a ribbon cutting ceremony for the Brooklyn Hispanic Chamber of Commerce Building, and at 5.40, in the Tishman Auditorium, persecuted scholars from the Middle East and Africa will take part in a panel discussion on global challenges to academic and intellectual freedom (Israeli participants have alas been boycotted). At 7.02 an earthquake will strike eastern Colombia, and at 7.05 Senator Barack Obama will speak to the Democratic Convention in West Virginia. At 9pm, unless the frozen rain pellets falling on the city and the minus twenty-six wind chill prevent him from getting to the lecture hall, Professor Haroun Mohammed will speak on the visible impact of global warming. Finally, we are told, at midnight precisely, a man claiming to be the Messiah will turn up in Bethlehem, carrying neither peace nor a sword but an explosive belt packed with dynamite and a promissory note from Osama bin Laden to be exchanged upon arrival in the Promised Land for seventy Jewish houris between the ages of seventeen and twenty-five, and a Nobel Peace Prize.

All this stirs in me the germ of an idea for an improvement to our school curriculum. In place of History – Future. Why not? It's likely to be less gloomy, less full of blood and failure, than the units taught at present. A space to dream, and hope, and yes, why not, to plan for dream and hope's fulfilment.

KNIGHT'S GAMBIT

Shortly after my arrival in the United States, I learned of a controversy that had considerably upset the literary world. A novel had appeared, taking its title – "Walking Shadows" – from a famous verse of Shakespeare: "Life is but a walking shadow, a poor player that struts and frets his hour upon the stage, and then is heard no more." The novel was set in one of the southern states, in Alabama I believe, in one of those mythical counties that take their name from the language of the local aboriginal peoples, and are generally unpronounceable. It told the story of one Sutpen Thomas, a civil war hero, and his somewhat complex family, employing various forms of stream of consciousness to tell the tale from different perspectives, including that of a genuine idiot, Sutpen's son Cuthbert.

Publication of the novel was met with a critical outcry, which no doubt assisted the publisher in moving well over a million copies in less than the first year. The claim that the novel was the work of Joe Christmas, the most successful quarterback ever to play for the Alabama Red Leaves, and the fact that "his novel" appeared at the end of a season when the Leaves had gone unvanquished for the first time in their history, no doubt contributed to the book's success as well; but the controversy wasn't over the false claim to authorship. This was quickly accepted by the reading public as proof of the merits of capitalism, market forces and free trade, and hailed as a shining symbol of the way in which anyone with a good idea could make a fortune in the United States. Christmas, and the ghost-writer, Faulkner Williams, were lauded for their entrepreneurial creativity, and many other would-be novelists and late-career athletes soon struck similar bargains.

Nor did the controversy lie in the fact that, on a superficial reading anyway, the text of "Walking Shadows" was identical to the 1929 novel "The Sound and the Fury" by William Faulkner. In fact, the texts are not identical at all. For one thing, Williams has changed the names of many characters. For another, and this was the crucial matter when the text was brought to court, Williams had made palpable improvements to the "original"; small and occasional improvements it is true, but improvements nonetheless. Within six weeks of the plagiarism allegation being dismissed in court, a further million copies of the book were sold. And this is where the controversy started. Bookshops and libraries throughout the United States are carrying copies of "Walking Shadows", but it has become impossible to locate a single copy of "The Sound and the Fury", and indeed, many critics already believe that that book has been permanently replaced, if not actually pulped.

Postscript: following the publication of the above article in "Dry

September" Literary Review (June 2007), I have learned that an improved version of the Mona Lisa, executed by a contemporary French artist claiming to be named Michel Platini, is to be placed in the gallery of the Louvre in Paris, less on the grounds that it's "better" than because the French believe their gallery should house a French "Mona Lisa" and not an Italian one, just as the Prado already houses a Spanish one, the Belgian a whole set of Mona Lisas on a single canvas by an artist claiming to be Magritte; and the Colombian a fine if slightly plump version by Fernando Botero. It isn't clear whether the Italians will request the return of the Leonardo model, as it has long been argued in that country that the original was itself a fake.

SELKIRK

In my 1978 essay "The Mythological Universe", reprinted at the end of this volume, I referred to Kafka's famous syllogism which states that "Had Robinson Crusoe never left the highest, or, more correctly, the most visible point of his island, he would soon have perished. But since, without paying any attention to passing ships and their feeble telescopes, he started to explore the whole island and take pleasure in it, he managed to keep himself alive, and was finally discovered after all, by a chain of causality that was, of course, logically inevitable."

Kafka understood that he was establishing a syllogism, but did he know that Robinson Crusoe was really Alexander Selkirk, a Scottish seaman who mutinied against his commander, William Dampier of the galleon Cinque Ports, and chose to abandon his ship when it left Fernandez Island? Did he know that February 2nd was the day on which, in 1709, Selkirk was rescued after four years on Fernandez Island? Did he know that Fernandez Island lies off the coast of Chile, that it's properly known as San Fernandez or even San Juan Fernandez island, and that it was here that the aboriginal peoples known as the Mosquito Men marooned their criminals, which fact may well have been in Defoe's mind when he placed his Crusoe there?

Selkirk, in fact, chose not the highest and most visible point of the island for his initial refuge, but the beach itself, fearing that the sounds he heard in the hinterland were wild beasts, and torn between the comforts of a seaside cave where sea shrimp were washed up constantly, and the torments of a seaside cave where rats gnawed at him when he was asleep and sea lions disputed with him ownership of the property. Kafka is correct however, in suggesting that he began to explore and enjoy the island, and might well have been rescued twice before he was; but on each occasion he hid from the visitors whose vessel had anchored on the island, because both were Spanish privateers, and he was British. Rather than rescue him, they would probably have killed him.

THE DISPUTATION OF TORTOSA

The year is 1413, the place Tortosa, a city in north-eastern Spain where Jews had lived longer than in any other town in all Iberia – the Romans knew it as Tartessus, where St Paul was shipwrecked, and previously it had been Tarshish, whither Jonah had tried, without success, to flee. When Tortosa lay in the Moslem sphere of influence, Jews were encouraged to work in agriculture and the maritime trades, to develop yeshivas, and in the 10th and 11th centuries Tortosa was the Sephardic Troyes, the epicentre of Judaic scholarship and poetry. Then, in 1391, Christianity marched south and drove the Moors out of Catalonia, began persecuting Jews, forcing them to accept baptism or martyrdom. The age of the marrano had begun, the Jews who pretended Christianity but kept their faith in secret. In 1492, when the expulsion of the Jews was proclaimed, it was from Tortosa that they boarded ship.

The Disputation of Tortosa was opened on February 7th, 1413. Its purpose was to prove beyond doubt, through the use of rational debate, that Christianity was the one true faith, that the coming of the Messiah Jesus had rendered Judaism obsolete. Its objective, beyond that proof, was to convince all Jews to accept baptism. Such disputations were commonplace in Europe in the Middle Ages. Amazingly, for such a learned and intellectual people, the Jews were never victorious, though draws have been recorded.

At Tortosa, the principal advocates on the Christian side were the anti-Pope Benedict XIII, whose presence was a mere formality, a Christian cleric by the name of Geronimo de Santa Fé, and the Jewish apostate Joshua Lorki. Four Rabbis spoke for the Jews: Zerachyah ha-Levi, Astruc ha-Levi, Joseph Albo and Mattathias ha-Yizchan. Of all the public disputations forced upon the mediaeval Jews, this at Tortosa went on the longest and was the most important. The nub of the argument was the nature of the Messiah and certain alleged abuses against Christianity in the Talmud.

Of the Jewish protagonists little is known, save only Joseph Albo, whose "*Sepher ha-Ikarim*", or "Book of Principles", is regarded as one of the major texts of Jewish philosophy in the middle ages; it based Judaism on the three foundation stones of divine existence, divine revelation, and divine justice, the latter being a balance of rewards and punishments.

As to the antagonists, the apologists for Christianity, they made an unusual trinity. The anti-Pope Benedict XIII was a learned man but quite obviously a lunatic, with several axes to grind, and more of them against the Christians than the Jews. His silence throughout the proceedings was exemplary. It's Lorki who is really interesting, and from whom we learn the true nature of both the disputation and that syllogistic cult of intellectual dialectics we call Judaism. Lorki was a Jew by birth and upbringing. He had been a physician for many years before he fell out with his own community; fearful of a repetition of the pogroms of 1391, he converted to Christianity in 1412, and immediately proved the sincerity of his conversion by calling for a public disputation with the Jews of Alcaniz, which was denied him, then of all of Aragon and Catalonia, which was granted. The third antagonist, the representative of Papal Orthodoxy Geronimo de Santa Fé, was actually Joshua Lorki himself, cognito by the name he took upon his baptism.

JOSEPH WAGENBACH

Joseph Wagenbach was a reclusive artist who left his native Germany in 1967, and took up residence at 105 Robinson Street, a single storey dwelling just west of Bathurst and Queen Street, in Toronto, a truly dilapidated house with a front lawn in urgent need of tending. In June 2006, after he suffered a debilitating stroke, "city officials uncovered a treasure trove of sculptured figures and sketches created by Wagenbach and a captivating biography that archivists hoped would lead to the city designating his house as a historical monument."[5] This treasure-trove included pillars of wax-covered objects, female figures with the heads of bunny rabbits, numerous drawings, dusty photographs, and a sealed shrine. Rumour had it that a former girlfriend had died in the house and was buried in the back garden.

Today a board outside the house informs the visitor that the Municipal Archives Assessment Unit is investigating the property as a potential "Legacy" site, and requests that all visitors – the house is open on Tuesdays through Sundays from 3 until 7pm - report to the field office, where they are met by Iris Häussler, the curator of this unusual exhibition, who is only too pleased to take you on a tour. Inside the house you are greeted by a coat hanger still bearing Herr Wagenbach's bowler hat and tweed jacket. On chairs and tables all around, as well as works of art, you will encounter teddy bears and dolls, covered in cement dust. The kitchen is filthy; hot plates covered with molten wax, tar and straw suggest these were not often used for preparing food. A dozen broom handles lean against a wall, stripped of their straw ends.

At the back of the house is the small gallery Herr Wagenbach created to store and perhaps one day show his works. Several sculpted nudes do not bear comparison with Rodin or with Henry Moore. Still more teddy bears, mounted on pedestals, lead the observer to wonder what trauma in his early life in Germany caused him to resort to art like this. Mirrors adorn the walls, granting a perspective on these works such as Cezanne sought to achieve at Mont St Victoire. Several columns of white flower pots stand glued together, rising into the ceiling like a Tower of Babel, and descending several feet down into the basement cellar through a hole cut in the floor. At the top, like the giant atop Jack's beanstalk, an attic room inhabited by an angelic figurine who sits astride the topmost flower pot.

But the attic is sealed. It's said that his muse, a woman by the name of Anna Neritti, deserted him in 1974, and he closed up the room where they'd slept, and blacked out the windows with the newspapers of the day

[5] http://www.nationalpost.com/news/story.html?id=239193a1-a542-47df-a6b7-0cc7fdadad1c&k=7209

of her desertion. A map of pre-war Germany dominates the attic, and the specific marking of a certain concentration camp suggests the source both of his reclusiveness and of his art. One has the same sense of walking over graves that one has at Anne Frank's house in Amsterdam, but for one important difference.

This is that there never was a man named Joseph Wagenbach. He is an invention of the curator, Iris Häussler, who set up the entire house, the sculptures, the teddy bears, the sealed attic, the flower pots, the maps, the brooms, the municipal notice in the garden, the whole elaborate hoax, and did so using grants from municipal, provincial and federal arts councils.

Footnotes:

How much better it would be if the National Post article itself turned out to be a hoax!

I have used the word "dilapidated", because that is what was in the National Post article. However, the etymological root is *lapis-lapidus* = "a stone", and this is a wooden dwelling. By definition a wooden dwelling cannot be dilapidated.

THE WOMAN IN THE NEXT SEAT

The woman in the next seat knows that she is beautiful. All men stare at her, and sometimes she resents their leers, and sometimes she takes delight from their delight, but it's utterly impossible for men to know which mood their stares will kindle. Merely they gaze, and hope.

The woman, who may be blonde or brunette, tall or short, understands that every man desires her, and that it's her destiny to be an object of desire before she is a woman with a name, a personality, a life, before she is a woman with desires of her own. This troubles her, but she's accustomed to it, and finally the advantages outweigh the disadvantages, and anyway it matters not a jot, provided she retains control. So the men around her fix their gaze, and she absorbs them. So the men around her yearn, and she is free to choose whether and on whom to bestow her favours.

The men, she knows from harsh experience, come in a multitude of guises, but behind the masks they are all the same one. They seek her body. Some wish to know her body, briefly, passionately, in order to be quickened by her beauty, as a light bulb is quickened by a wave of electricity, only to die out when the current is switched off. Some wish to inhabit her body in order to destroy it, because they cannot bear to witness their own ugliness; for ugliness is relative, yet ugliness increases in the instant of destroying. Some wish to sleep beside her body, because it's warm, and cradling, and less solitary than making love alone; but she knows that they would still be making love alone. Some wish just to use her body for their own gratification, to notch another number on the blackboard of their conquests, to embrace her like a trophy. Some wish to be ornamented by her body, to wear her as they would a sapphire or a gold watch or a designer suit. Some wish to make her body the subject of their dreams, the untouchable enigma whom they have encountered once, and longed for through eternity. Some wish to make her body the object of their fantasies, engraving her upon their memories so they can take her home with them, to use her like an air-doll in the solitary desolation of the night. Some wish to possess her body, as they do their Persian cat, their Porsche, their season ticket.

All these men are different, yet all these men are the same. All in their own ways have imagined entering her body, and if they've bothered to ask her name it was only out of politeness, or as an aid to memory, or as a tactic in the great game of seduction. Her name, her personality, her life, are incidental. To each one she is just her body, and what excites them is her body's impact on their own body, her capacity to stimulate their desire. To each one, were she to get up and move to another seat, were she to be replaced by another creature of equal looks, it would be as if nothing had

157

altered.

So she sits, and ponders. She too has desires, and perhaps, perhaps, one man among all these will treat her as herself, will desire her for her and not for him. This man? Could it be this man, the one who has opened his notebook and is writing down these very lines? Could it, perhaps, be him? Do these lines that he's writing signify that he's the one who understands, he whom destiny has appointed for her – or is the act of writing simply his seduction technique, his point of relativity to her body?

She sits, ponders, hopes, doubts. He who has written will not speak. It is for her to speak. But experience makes her so wary, so unsure. And the silence holds hands with the silence. But the man and the woman do not touch.

And now the man has put away his notebook, resigned himself to leaving without speaking to her, given up all hope. And the woman in the next seat knows that she has missed her chance.

THE FORMER STUDENT

The former student returned, after several years, to his alma mater – accounts of the story do not record what subject he had studied, but in the opinion of this author it might have been almost any subject: perhaps the reader will decide.

Entering his tutor's study he found it empty, but he couldn't resist the pleasure of leafing through the pile of examination papers on the desk. To his amazement, this year's examination was identical, in every degree, to the paper he had sat a decade earlier.

While he was browsing, the tutor at last came in, and after much hand-shaking and reminiscing, the former student expressed aloud his astonishment at the repetition of the paper.

"Why are you so surprised?" the tutor smiled. "Don't you know that we set the very same examination paper every year? There are, after all, only a strictly limited number of pertinent questions, and they remain eternally the same. But the answers, the answers; they are always different."

THE IMMACULATE FAILURE

Over the years I have presented this parable in a number of different versions, with different sages offering the lesson, with different mountains as the goal, and even, on some occasions, with seas or deserts, symphonies or philosophical treatises, jungle expeditions or worthy idealisms replacing the allegorical mountains. Each version is nonetheless the same. It goes, on this occasion, as follows:

"After a certain point" - the Sherpa Ten-Sing is said to have told Sir Edmund Hilary – "you have climbed so high that vertigo makes it impossible to look down, and so, for your own safety, you are obliged to fix your eyes on the summit, and hasten to reach there. It's a question of struggling towards that point."

Over dinner, the philosopher Con-Fu-Se explained the parable thus:

The first man lives in a valley surrounded by low hills. He sets himself the goal of climbing the highest of those hills, and one day he manages it. Reaching the top he meets a second man, who points out to him a second range of hills, invisible from the lower valley, rising above this one and making it appear quite flat. Mocking the first man's achievement, he sets out to climb the highest of those hills. At the top he encounters a third man, who informs him that his ambition was to travel to this point from the valley on the other side, and here he is now, gloating on his achievement. Together the two men look upwards to the high mountains above them, and to a solitary figure, seemingly inert just below the cloud-line.

"Ah," one of them says, "when a man tries to climb that high he's bound to fail, because that mountain has no summit. That's the mountain of the gods, whose peak is infinite. We've set ourselves grand but sensible ambitions, and realised them. Let us drink to our success."

High up among the peaks the fourth man is unaware of all this. His eyes are bent upwards through the clouds towards his unattainable goal. Cold has bitten his fingers to the bones, frozen his heart practically motionless. Struggling forward, he drags himself closer and closer towards his own death.

"It is this," Con-Fu-Se smiled, "that I call the Immaculate Failure."

DEATH

None of you has ever seen me face to face, though many think you know who I am, and many in your vanity believe that you have seen me, and - true enough - there are those of you who have unwittingly brushed the shoulder of my shadow. In your imagination I am that monkish figure in a famous Ingmar Bergman movie, with whom a soldier played his life out for a game of chess. Lovely image - great movie - but alas it isn't me. In your Art I am the Grim Reaper, skeletal face, armed with a scythe. Or Old Father Time, passing more slowly and lugubriously than a Lords Test Match, inevitable as an English defeat. But these are not me either. Though I am, as you've by now rightly deciphered, Death.

Think of me as your friend, not your enemy. I do what I do without malevolence, because this is the purpose for which I was made. Imagine how much more intolerable your overcrowded cities would become, if there weren't a regular and natural cull by means of old age, peradventure and disease? Imagine living to be several hundred years old, blind, infirm, decrepit, unable to speak or hear, incontinent. Beyond a certain point, eternal life isn't really such a boon. That's when I become your salvation, your best friend.

I have – I'm fully willing to admit it - perpetrated many a terrible deed. Though not the ones that you might think, perhaps. I've never caused a famine, nor a drought - only men do that, by their politics, or their greed. I've never made war - there too, men bear the responsibility. Yet every year, in Europe alone, I strike down something in the order of six million, and every death is necessary, right and natural. You cannot accuse me of any sin, any misdemeanour, any immorality. I mentioned the figure six million, and this was deliberate, to illustrate my point. Every year six million die, but no one calls for war crimes trials to punish me, no one calls on me for reparations. But that six million, the six million I have evoked by naming that symbolic number. Blame God if you must. Blame men. They were not my doing.

AN ADDITIONAL CHAPTER

Browsing through the public library recently I came upon a small volume entitled "An Anthology Of Essays On Modern Literature" (Rebaf & Rebaf 1952. ed. David Goodhope), and discovered, in the midst of this prolix and irrelevant work, what was presumably an error in the printing - a critique of "The Castle" by D.H. Lawrence. I have said "presumably an error", and this is deliberate, for in re-reading both Kafka and Lawrence I have found evidence to support the view that it may not be an error at all. I do not propose a full analysis of the subject in order to demonstrate this, but merely a few suggestions which will allow the reader to judge the matter for himself.

"The Castle" was written in 1922, and broadly it tells of a man alienated in a foreign country, struggling against that country's political hierarchy, trying both to comprehend it and to break through its obduracy. This general theme is also central to Lawrence's novel "Kangaroo", written in Australia at exactly the same time. Lawrence described his life at this period as being "a savage pilgrimage", and his novels as "thought adventures" - the allegorical journey of K and the narrative momentum of "The Castle" exemplify both of these notions, while the chapter "Nightmare" in "Kangaroo" clearly gives us the seed of the other claustrophobic tale. K's lover Frieda is undoubtedly a portrait of Lawrence's own wife, Frieda von Richthofen, while K himself must be seen, like so many of Lawrence's central characters, as autobiographical, or at least automythological (is K perhaps, also, an oblique reference to the initial letter of "Kangaroo"?). The inconsistency of styles between the two works may be attributable to the fact that they were written in different languages, German and English; nonetheless a glance at Lawrence's many letters to both his mother- and sister-in-law testify to the writer's proficiency in both tongues...

Ultimately "The Castle" belongs as much to Lawrence as it does to Kafka (and even more to Rabbi Nachman of Bratzlav). Our view of the work must be radically altered when we discover the true identity of its author, and likewise our view of Lawrence must change when we learn of this additional chapter in his life's work. But something else changes too. What if the printing error had given us Flaubert instead of Lawrence, or if, in naming Kafka, it had intended a different Kafka from the one who wrote "The Trial" and the tormented letters to Felice Bauer?

Every word implies the universe, every book belongs to the universal Book of Literature, of which it is but a single line. In the same way these words are not mine - Pushkin and Stendhal, among others, have used them before me. The page is indifferent to the signature at its foot. To write is to participate in a Cabal, to juggle the ciphers with which our human consciousness expresses and manifests itself, through which the psyche (some would say God, or the Muse) may be given substance. The book belongs, not to its author, but to Man, and to language, and to tradition. Translated into Greek or Chinese - as it is here translated into English from the Hebrew - this essay would be transformed entirely, and transformed again if I were to sign it with my real name, which is Pliny, which is Shakespeare, which is Joyce.

Quoted from Chaim Nachman Bialik: Diaries 1939-45

EPILOGUE: THE BESTIARY

Primo Levi, in a masterful essay ("Other People's Trades", p27ff), has described the processes and limitations involved in the invention of an animal. He notes that "to invent from nothing an animal that can exist is an almost impossible feat", and then goes on to cite some remarkable attempts to prove this proposition false. He quotes the chimera - a hybrid of lion, snake and goat - which has come to symbolise "all vain hopes", including, presumably, that of inventing an animal, and that of proving the impossibility of doing so. He refers, inevitably, to Borges' "Book Of Imaginary Beings", which fatuously he re-translates as "The Manual Of Fantastic Zoology". He mentions the centaur, and demonstrates the imaginative plausibility but biological implausibility of such a beast. He then describes an exercise in an Italian school in which pupils were invited to contribute their own phantasmagorical creations; and analyses the techniques involved: the lack of originality in the apparently original; the tendency to borrow existing animal forms and to reassemble them in patterns and permutations apparently discarded or overlooked by evolution (Levi is scrupulous in saying "evolution" and not "God") - beasts with numerous limbs, eyes, members; mammals with redistributed parts; a mere "recombining of already known building elements".

In describing some of these creatures - the Executioner which eats only human flesh and fruit trees, and hides in fear of the other horrible animals described by the other children; the Lymph Dinosaur; the enormous Neck-Giant which wood-cutters use to saw wood; the animal with the unpronounceable eighteen syllable name which eats with its tail while its head stands guard; the Leptorontibus which has no bones but is held upright by its nervous system; the Mostrumgaricus which, like Achilles, is invulnerable save for one flaw, in its case fear of the disease called gloomititus; the Coco, which comes from China but lives in a house in Turin and smokes a pipe; the Cibercus, which is made of cream and dines on mice and chocolate - Levi shows us how the pupils have resorted to traditional archetypes in devising their bestiary and by implication suggests how we, his readers, may expand the encyclopaedia by imitating God, or rather evolution, or perhaps just Mary Shelley, ourselves.

To this unlikely zoo I now to invite you to contribute your own inventions, which, with the goodwill of my publisher, will be collected, sorted, sifted, awarded prizes, and then published as soon as sufficient of sufficient quality come together to merit a collection...

APPENDIX: THE MYTHOLOGICAL UNIVERSE

An Essay In Toccata Form

First Movement

1.

a) The Oxford English Dictionary - is there a higher authority? - defines a myth as "a purely fictitious narrative, usually involving supernatural persons, and embodying popular ideas on natural phenomena".

b) The phrase "purely fictitious" may cause offence, casting doubt as it does on the historical authenticity of, let us say, Buddha, or Jesus, or Shakespeare, or the Babylonian Titan Utnapishtim.

c) "Supernatural persons" is likewise curious - who was ever more human than Zeus, who less godlike than Anansi? - since the term must be flexible enough to incorporate both Leonardo da Vinci and Mozart.

d) And as to "embodying popular ideas on natural phenomena" - does this include that mystical leap of faith the "Big Bang" and that atavistic superstition, its existence still unproven by logic, reason or science, which men call the psyche or the mind?

2.

a) The word "narrative" is thus all that remains of our definition.

b) If we accept it, then we accept that the Bible is a collection of myths, the Edda likewise, so too the Epic of Gilgamesh, the Diaries of Samuel Pepys, and the novels of Thomas Hardy.

c) But we must also accept that so too is Descartes' "Discourse on the Method" and Einstein's exegesis of the formula $E=MC^2$, a narrative song-cycle such as Wagner's "Ring" (a Myth of Myths, strictly speaking) and a narrative painting such as Brueghel's "Hunters in the Snow".

d) To tell the story of a human life is to recite a narrative, and all of us in telling of our own lives inexorably indulge in the fictitious. Ergo all human life is mythological, even, perhaps, while we are still living it.

e) We are not likely to make much progress down this cul de sac.

3.

a) A myth - or a work of Art, of Literature, of Science, of philosophical speculation - is an attempt to construct an allegorical model of the Universe, a paradigm. Such a model is never - to use Rilke's term - "the Thing itself". Rather it's the Thing's shadow, its echo, its reflection; and it may be as vast and complicated as a name, or as simple as a doctoral thesis.

b) If one were God, one could name the Thing, and in the very act of naming it bring it into existence. "Let there be Love - and there was Love."

c) But we are the descendants of Adam, the magic-less, who only gave names to all Things which already existed, in order to denote them, not to create them.

d) When we name Love (or Glass, or Plato), we do so only to evoke it, and our evocation assumes a community of understanding amongst all namers, a shared acceptance of general meaning behind which lies a whole universe - I use the term advisedly, for each of us is himself a universe - of personal, unshareable meanings.

e) I name the Light, and it's understood that I'm denoting the sun's rays; but I'm also thinking of the disc of Akhenaton, the writings of Faulkner and Tennyson, of this lamp that stands beside me on the desk where I'm writing, of the girl in the shop where I bought it, and of that other girl whom she resembled, who I loved a decade ago when I first encountered her in the pages of Count Leo Tolstoy...

f) This is my personal universe, and it, and the Light, are my personal myths. But though I can name them in their last detail, I cannot finally render them up to you (errors, too, are inevitable; as for example your thinking I meant by Glass the obscurantist American composer, when in fact I simply meant that lustrous fusing of sand and potash that fills our windows and doubles as a mirror). At most I can describe them to you in a narrative form - all narrative is fictitious - but even that is necessarily incomplete. The allegorical world reveals far less than it leaves hidden.

4.

a) To paint Jesus resurrected is not the Resurrection ("ceci n'est pas une pipe"). To pronounce the name of God is not to manifest Him in the flesh. To construct a table one may use letters or numbers or wood. To elaborate the physiology of Love does not require a kiss.

166

b) There is the life, and then there is the telling of the life, which is much less, but entails and describes much more, for living is an act of direct apprehension, contact, passage, but the telling - a rendering into fiction by process of selection, omission, interpretation - is merely a naming of incidents now stripped of apprehension, contact, passage.

c) To describe is to resort to metaphors, myths, allegorical models. Even this essay is not the universe, but only the allegorical model of an allegorical model of the universe - a myth of a myth. Indeed, some might argue that even the universe is not the universe, but only a paradigm, that we are the inhabitants, not of the Thing itself, the actual universe which exists elsewhere, in the mind of God, but only of the Name, which God uttered to denote us: a myth fashioned in the imagination of an unnamed and unnameable divinity. We should never allow ourselves to overlook the fact that, if God created us but God does not exist, then nor do we.

5.

a) In his "Library At Babel", Borges imagines the ultimate paradigm - a model of the universe which is equivalent in every way to the actual Universe:

"The library is unlimited and cyclical. If an eternal traveller were to cross it in any direction, after centuries he would see that the same volumes were repeated in the same disorder (which, thus repeated, would be an order: the Order)."

b) Unattainable Unity, circles unfurling into spirals, disorder arranged with such apparently methodical madness that it takes on the appearance of designed order, myths that explain myths but which are themselves inexplicable, metaphors of such ridiculous complexity, or such unfathomable simplicity, that they obscure even themselves - perhaps the great mistake of God was not to imagine that He could create a perfect Universe, but to imagine that He could create anything at all using a material as volatile, as incalculable, as Chaos.

c) Borges' library is a metaphor encompassing a myth; the books in that library are myths composed of metaphors. And in the same way the Universe is itself but a metaphor, a myth conceived by a mythical God that equally contains the mythical godhead as a metaphor of its own (questionable?) existence.

6.

a) In a letter to Lady Ottoline Morrel, dated May 1916, D.H. Lawrence wrote that:

"When one is shaken to the very depths, one finds reality in the unreal world. At present my real world is the world of my inner soul, which reflects on the novel I write. The outer world is there to be endured, it is not real - neither the outer life."

b) Because Lawrence, who had more profound things to say than any other English writer of the 20th century, was also in the all-too-frequent habit of spouting unmitigated nonsense, one may feel justified in treating the above with some scepticism. I do not, however, propose entering into a debate with the ghost of a dead genius (which is to say, the spirit of a spirit): my quotation is illustrative, not dialectical. I am intrigued only by Lawrence's assumption of the separate existences of a "real" and of an "unreal" world, of the possibility of differentiating between the two.

c) To me, a character in the novel I am reading may be as real, sometimes more real, than the unknown stranger whom chance has seated next to me in the train.

d) To me, when an idea forms in my - where do ideas live? in the brain, that offal-bag of blood and tissue? in the intellect, as unproven in its physical existence as are the soul and mind? – it's as real as the pen with which I record it, the words that I use to express it, and indeed the virtual reality of cyberspace in which I keep it filed.

e) To me, when I'm asleep, there is no other reality than the world of my dream, just as, when I hear the chanting of the muezzin from the loud-speaker in the nearby mosque, there is no other reality than the world of Islam. (The muezzin, however, is pure illusion, for the voice is pre-recorded.)

f) To me, the idea of a naked, feeling soul is as implausible as John Donne's "naked, thinking heart", and yet I have no difficulty accepting the myth of a lucid, rationalising mind.

b) To me, it seems incredible that people can believe in God, and yet I cannot imagine a Universe in which people did not hold such a belief.

7.

a) When the Emperor Titus entered the Holy of Holies in the Jewish Temple in Jerusalem, he was astonished to come upon the seeming absence of a deity in which, of course, he didn't anyway believe. Yet he understood this emptiness to be sacred, and so he ordered that it be transported in triumph back to Rome.

b) When the surgeon Harvey first dissected a human brain - a Holy of Holies in itself - he was unable to explain the seeming absence of thought, of memory, of imagination. His writings speak of the cerebellum as "a temple". His ethical observations on cerebral anatomy and dissection infer a sense of sacredness.

c) To me, a paradox, an irony, such as the above, can be entirely tenable, despite its intellectual felicity, for the simple pleasure, the purely aesthetic satisfaction that it gives. After all, a baby doesn't need to justify its existence, even if it's ugly, or retarded, or deformed, or full of lies and falsehoods - why then must ideas?

8.

I hear one man preaching the doctrines of some religious sect, another the dogma of some political faction, and I recognise that their respective roads make them the most bitter of enemies, though their shared goals ought to bind them in eternal brotherhood.

9.

a) When the mind conceives the idea of a non-existent form, one that cannot actually be realised, it nonetheless adds one more phenomenon to this overcrowded Universe.

c) When the mind conceives the idea of a non-existent form, one that cannot actually be realised, and thereby adds one more phenomenon to this overcrowded Universe, it also perpetrates a blasphemy against that other non-existent form, the Almighty and Only-Permitted Creator: God.

10.

a) The unknown is "real", just as is the unknowable.

b) The "Bhagavad-Gita", which is a myth composed of metaphors, informs us that:

"The Unreal never is; the Real never is not."

which may be a contradiction in terms, or simply a convolutedly ungrammatical way of stating the obvious.

c) To some people the world is a process of extension, and each step forward into the unknown reveals a new mystery. To others it's a process of reduction, in which every instant may be knowable and attributable to the workings of a vast organised system. But it's always the same world that they are describing.

d) De Sade has written, in "Justine", that:

"The mirror sees the man as beautiful, the mirror loves the man; another mirror sees the man as frightful, and hates him; and it is always the same being who produces the impressions."

In all these matters I remain agnostic.

*

Second Movement

1.

a) By chance, a few days ago, I came upon a deck of Tarot cards; by chance the first card I turned over was the Wheel Of Fortune. I cannot say that this coincidence surprised me in the slightest.

b) Nor did those in an essay by André Maurois that I came upon recently (the essay was about the Argentinian writer Jorge Luis Borges, some of whose stories I happened to be reading at the time).

"For example, Pascal wrote: 'Nature is an infinite sphere whose centre is everywhere, whose circumference is nowhere'...in Giordano Bruno (1584): 'We can assert with certainty that the Universe is all centre, or that the centre of the Universe is everywhere and its circumference nowhere.' But Giordano Bruno had been able to read in a 12th century theologian, Alain de Lille, a formulation borrowed from the 'Corpus Hermeticum' (3rd century): 'God is an intelligible sphere whose centre is everywhere and whose circumference is nowhere.'

2.

a) Borges delights in these coincidences - he says elsewhere that "what we call chance is simply our ignorance of the complex machinery of causality" - because he finds in them those very paradoxes and absurdities which not only make up the Universe, but which are the Universe (or God, or Nature).

b) The "real" world - I am paraphrasing Borges; which is to say, I'm offering a fictitious narrative of his views; which is to say, what I'm now explaining isn't the ideas of Borges at all, but a myth purporting to contain them - is simply...let us suggest some allegorical models:

* an infinite possibility containing an infinite number of further possibilities, all of which exist simultaneously, none of which can be fully realised;

* a vast Chinese Doll in which every layer is of the same size;

* a magic circle enlarged into an impossibly labyrinthine mandala;

* a spectacular hypothesis posited by a highly imaginative and whimsical God;

* a film-version of a stage-play, projected in a mirror;

* a universe-sized map of the universe.

Any one of these, or none, or all of them.

c) For Borges, each of those phrases in Maurois' essay (which turned out to be a quote from Borges himself; and which essay would itself turn up, several years later and in an English translation, as the preface to another collection of his writings) is in fact the same phrase, repeated by different people at different times for different purposes - apparently varied but in fact the same phrase.

d) What is fascinating isn't simply the chance repetition of a number of words, not simply the way in which a coincidence suggests or even implies that God, Nature and the Universe may be one and the same thing (what pantheist, after all, would disagree?), but the thread that links them, the Unifying Principle: that repository in which Jung believed he had detected the image of the collective unconscious: the eternal recurrence combined with the eternal flux; the apparent simultaneity extending over periods of several hundred years.

e) To my mind, this is what we mean when we speak of "reality" and "unreality" (to my mind, though not necessarily to D.H. Lawrence's, let alone the Buddha's!). It's simply a question of perspective. Because the first principle of the Universe is that there is no first principle of the Universe. All is paradox. What we call order may simply be an eternally consistent chaos.

*

Third Movement

1.

a) An event that is unusual, even implausible, takes place, and we term it an accident, and ascribe to it proof of the random and arbitrary nature of the universe.

b) Later the event is repeated, and we term it a coincidence.

c) By the third occasion we are beginning to suspect that it isn't random or arbitrary after all, but normal, natural.

d) By the fourth occasion - which we anticipated - we take its inevitability for granted.

e) By the fifth we can deduce the logic and the symmetry of the Universe.

f) By the sixth we have established a Universal Law.

g) The seventh occasion - a variant - is the exception which proves the rule.

h) The fact that the eighth occasion never arises is not disproof, but merely an event that is unusual, even implausible.

"To accept the possibility of accidents is to deny Fatalism; to expect accidents is Fatalistic."

2.

a) An event that is unusual, even implausible, takes place, and we term it a miracle, and ascribe to it proof of the existence of God.

b) Later the event is repeated, and we accept the coincidence which both reinforces and undermines the miraculous.

c) By the third occasion we are beginning to suspect that it isn't divinely inspired after all, but normal, natural.

d) By the fourth occasion - which we anticipated - we take its inevitability for granted.

e) By the fifth we can claim an insight into the logic and symmetry of the Divine Plan.

f) By the sixth we have established His Universal Law.

g) The seventh occasion - a variant - is an example of Free Will.

h) The fact that the eighth occasion never arises is not only not disproof, but in fact a verification of the omnipotence of God, a call to us for patience, faith and piety, for have not the Prophets ensured us that the eighth occasion will indeed arise, when the Messiah comes?

"He who believes in miracles is an imbecile. He who does not is an atheist."

3.

Both quotations are from the 18th century Hasidic Rebbe Wolfe of Zhitomir.

*

4th Movement

1.

a) It is recorded that Abraham Lincoln had, for his personal secretary, a man by the name of Kennedy; and that John F. Kennedy had, for his personal secretary, a man by the name of Lincoln. Abraham Lincoln's assassin, Booth, was born in 1840; Kennedy's assassin, Oswald, in 1940. Lincoln was elected President in 1860, Kennedy in 1960. Lincoln was killed in a theatre and his assassin arrested in a nearby warehouse; Kennedy's assassin fired from the roof of a warehouse and was arrested in a nearby theatre. Both assassins were themselves murdered while awaiting execution; both Presidents were succeeded by Southern Democratic senators named Johnson.

b) It is logical to suppose that all time takes place simultaneously (after all, if it can be lunchtime in London and suppertime in Sydney, why can it not be CE in Paris and BCE in Tokyo, or both the 18th and the 21st centuries - as, for most orthodox Jews, it is?), that even now Brutus is plotting the assassination of Julius Caesar - an assassination whose similarities with those of Lincoln and Kennedy I shall not waste time illustrating - that even now Shakespeare is recording the event in a play, that even now a company of actors is performing the play on a stage on the steps of the Capitol in Rome. It is logical in the most pristine sense of that word. In mathematical logic (mathematology, to coin a term), two plus two equals four; in theosophical logic (theology - the rational, academic study of blind faith) two plus two equals One, as all equations equal One, now and for evermore, amen. Which logic?

*

2.

a) Time - whose centre is everywhere and whose circumference is nowhere - is at best a metaphor, at worst a syllogism. If we use the flawed allegorical model of GMT it's only because, without it, our world would lack stability. In the same way that mediaeval Europe required the world to remain flat and the universe geocentric, so we require two plus two to equal four (is this the same or a different four from the one which minus two times minus two also equal?), and twelve noon in London to equal nine pm in Sydney.

b) Our carefully conditioned consciousness of "reality" enables us to build a raft against the chaos. But tamper with that carefully constructed mythological Universe, and our illusion of a "real" and an "unreal" world is immediately refuted - like mediaeval man, if we sail out too far, we risk falling off the edge. Like Prometheus, to give our lives meaning, to *be* Prometheus, we need a rock to which we can be chained.

c) And yet the model is tampered with, refuted, constantly. When science advances beyond the point where the layman can comprehend it, then it is no longer possible for him to distinguish it from magic (or to know whether it is black magic, or white).

d) Perhaps the only significant difference between our epoch and previous ones is that we did not burn Einstein to death for doing to the twentieth century (the fourteenth, according to Islam) what Giordano Bruno did to the sixteenth (which the Jews count as the fifty-fourth). Yet even that is only partially true, for we didn't burn his books, but we did transform his discoveries into the means of burning several hundred thousand Giordano Brunos - but that must be the subject of another essay.

*

Fifth Movement

1.

a) *"Had Robinson Crusoe never left the highest, or, more correctly, the most visible point of his island, he would soon have perished. But since, without paying any attention to passing ships and their feeble telescopes, he started to explore the whole island and take pleasure in it, he managed to keep himself alive, and was finally discovered after all, by a chain of causality that was, of course, logically inevitable."*

b) I doubt, in fact, whether Kafka sincerely believes in this "chain of causality" of which he speaks. It was, nonetheless, inevitable that Robinson Crusoe should have been found, just as, if he had not been found, that too would have been inevitable. The chains, the real chains, are those of logic, not causality. Belief is always a syllogism, founded on two (or more) conflicting truths.

c) We say that "seeing is believing" and, on the premise that the multiplication of two negatives invariably creates a single positive (a statement that may well be true in mathematics but, alas, is all too rarely true in life), conclude that the deluded belief in having seen an apparition, a mirage, confirms an authentic vision. The statement "the ghost must have been there because I saw it" is equally as true and equally as false as the statement "the ghost could not have been there because I didn't see it". Nonetheless, both presuppose the existence of ghosts, whether in "reality", or "in the mind". If the ghost was there, ergo ghosts exist; and if it wasn't there - ah, then it must have been somewhere else.

d) By the same logic God must exist, because if God did not exist, then whose existence is it, pray, that I am disputing and denying now? My denial of His existence presupposes and confirms His necessarily existing.

e) The idea of God is no less real than God Himself. To name God is to bring Him into existence.

f) Delusion is a mental state, as is dream, or thought, or memory, or imagination. All things exist "only in the mind", whether tangible or imaginary, for the mind - which of all things does not exist - *is* reality.

f) Descartes has shown that the existence of Things depends upon our consciousness of them; "real" or "unreal", they exist precisely because they are "only in the mind" - be they ghosts, or beings from another planet, or the conviction that Britain is a democratic state, or God, or your reflection in the mirror, or the Universe itself, or the man next-door, or indeed this essay.

g) All reality, according to the Hindus, is illusion. Perhaps the universe is only a ghost, which inhabits the delusions of a demented deity.

*

Sixth Movement

1.

Trotsky has written, in "Literature and Revolution":

"Alongside the twentieth century there lives the tenth, the thirteenth. A hundred million people use electricity, and still believe in the magic power of signs and exorcisms. The Pope broadcasts over the radio the miraculous transformation of water into wine. Movie stars go to mediums. Aviators who pilot miraculous machines created by Man's genius wear amulets on their sweaters..."

2.

We "see" a ghost, but we refuse to believe that it is there, we insist that "there must be some deeper psychological explanation" - and we believe the psychological explanation even though we understand the psyche quite as little as we do the ghost, even though, were we to cut open the brain and search every last millimetre of it, we would be unable to "see" the psyche in which the ghost apparently lives. Ah, but we *want* to believe in the psyche, and we *want* to disbelieve in ghosts.

3.

a) In place of knowledge - which turned out to be entirely suspect - Man has appropriated myth. In place of authentic truth, Man has appropriated subjective preference.

b) In place of the myth of God, Man has appropriated the Divine Myth of Man.

c) In place of the Unknown, Man has appropriated - no, perpetrated - the myth of the Unconscious (an infinite sphere whose centre is everywhere and whose circumference is nowhere).

d) But the explanation ultimately fails, and all we actually do is not explain, but explain away. For myths never explain "reality" or "unreality"; they are merely an adequate metaphor. Today the myth of God is no longer satisfactory to our needs and purposes, and so we have replaced it - with another myth that equally fails to explain "reality" and "unreality", that is equally unsatisfactory to our needs and purposes. For the subconscious is as mystifying and as terrifying to us as God was previously. The deepest, darkest, most disconcerting corners of the human consciousness, those we will only visit after paying Dr Cerberus to row us across the psychiatric river on his couch-boat, are the self-same Hades that Dante visited with Virgil, that Orpheus harrowed in search of Eurydice, and in which King Saul pursued the bandit David.

e) The priest has changed his mask, but the face behind the mask remains the same. The change of metaphor does nothing but offer an alternative illusion as though it were an advance in knowledge and understanding. Behind the mask, we remain in the same enormous ignorance. Psychoanalysis is simply the confession-booth of atheism.

g) So the unknown remains unknown, the inexplicable remains unexplained. But the myth also remains the myth, and it's available for reinterpretation by each contemporary shaman. Aeschylus' Oedipus is not the same as Dr Freud's, nor Martin Luther's Jesus the same as St Augustine's, yet both inhabit their own contemporary realities, our own contemporary realities. Perhaps this is as much as we can ever hope to know.

*

Seventh Movement

1.

a) For most of us, this will not suffice. Being phenomenologists - which is to say, grounded in empirical science - being dialectical materialists, we refuse even to countenance the hypothesis that the two myths (the old and the new testaments, so to speak), the two metaphors, God and the subconscious, may very well be One and the same.

b) And yet. We laugh at the primitive witch-doctors, and we accept the incomprehensible quasar without batting an eyelid, without realising that "scientist" may well be nothing more than a pseudonym for "shaman".

c) We watch one man pull a rabbit out of a hat and we call him a magician; we watch another man pull the formula $E=MC^2$ out of a philosophical hat, and we call him a scientific genius (a simple proof of $E=MC^2$ which Einstein probably never thought of: when $E=18$ based on $M=2$ and $C=3$; Maths for 9 year olds – ah, not *that* $E=MC^2$! But perhaps also: not *that* God, not *that* Reality, not *that* Unconscious, not *that* Love). And between the two, between the shaman and the shaman, between the magician and the scientist: what on earth are we to do with a man like Yuri Geller?

d) In fact, technology and magic are much closer than we imagine, only something about the empirical nature of our minds wishes to associate the comprehensible with the true and call it "real", the incomprehensible with the false and call it "unreal" - as though these two (truth and reality, falsehood and unreality) were fragments of a whole, interdependent to the point that one cannot exist without the other.

e) The ghost, in fact, is no more real and no more unreal than this essay - both may be seen, yet both are entirely figments, creations, inventions, of the human imagination. The error is the same one Keats made in that glorious moment of wishful thinking when he wrote that "Truth is Beauty, Beauty Truth, that is all ye know on Earth, and all ye need to know". In point of fact, Truth is almost invariably Illusion, Illusion Truth, and Beauty merely one of its rare but myriad manifestations.

f) I imagine a future in which rockets bearing little green men to Earth from outer space are as commonplace and as free of demoniacal superstitions as are, shall we say, televisions and computers today. Nonetheless I do not believe in flying saucers, nor in ghosts, and would not, *even if I were to see one*. I can hear myself saying it: "there has to be some sort of rational explanation." (Yes, but I - just like you, I'm sure – I'm not even capable of giving a rational explanation of the computer and the television: they exist for my use, not my understanding.)

2.

a) I look at Monet's paintings of his garden, which I have also visited, and I'm convinced that the paintings are "truer" than the garden itself, even while the latter is the only authentic reality of the garden.

b) I imagine an object suspended impossibly in space - a flower, say, or an aeroplane - and I posit the not-irrational supposition that it's hanging there simply because gravity is defiable by artistic truth.

c) I imagine a group of philosophers who produce a complete encyclopaedia of a fictional world, and then circulate the manuscript, claiming that this other world not only exists but has, as its primary objective, the total conquest of our world. Some years later scientific enquiry and technological advance reach a point at which the encyclopaedia may be read as an extraordinarily accurate account of our world. But in the meantime the fraud - or practical joke - of the philosophers has been revealed. Or has it?

d) All truth, even axiomatic truth, is ultimately speculation waiting to be disproved, just as all reality is ultimately a mask, an illusion, a hypothesis. Knowledge is simply the present state of our uncertainty, waiting to be reduced.

3.

a) If it were to be discovered that "Madame Bovary" had not been written by Flaubert, but by George Sand?

b) If it were discovered that "Hedda Gabbler" wasn't a fiction at all, but an authentic, fact by fact transposition of certain events in the life of a real woman, but that Ibsen had changed one detail: that the original Hedda did not commit suicide?

c) If it were discovered that the entire Apollo moon-project was an elaborate hoax perpetrated for the purposes of morale and propaganda, that Man had never left the Earth's atmosphere let alone walked on the surface of the moon; that the whole project had been simulated, using the most advanced technological wizardry, filmed on location in Iceland or in the depths of the Judean desert?

d) If it were discovered that a man had turned up in Jerusalem, whose face was a perfect facsimile of the one on the Turin Shroud, who, under hypnotic regression, gave a full account of one of his several former lives on Earth, as the mortal Jesus Christ?

e) "Truth," Lawrence Durrell has written, "is independent of fact. It does not mind being disproved. It is already dispossessed in utterance."

*

Coda

1.

a) To pursue the notion of Absolute Truth is to practice dilettantism, to transform philosophy into an endless "Glass Bead Game".

b) In the end we have, as certainty, only the Machiavellian "effectual truth" - that which is useful to us.

c) And which truth is that? This is simple: the only truth that is useful to us is the truth that is useful to us - the truth which recognises its own illusoriness, the vacuum upon which it is built, the fact that, doubtless, it will later be shown up as a falsehood, the fact that it cannot ultimately provide any answer at all, but only serve a useful if ephemeral purpose as symbol, metaphor – myth.

d) The great Truths professed by one generation are invariably shown, in the next, to be at best partial, at worst false. All truth is provisional. What seem to be answers prove to be nothing but the curious misphrasing of further questions.

e) Yet the world cannot function without these myths, without these necessary illusions. Nor does a truth that is disproved automatically become a lie, does it become any less "real" for having been discredited. Philosophy is the pursuit of the unfindable. The goal is absolute knowledge. The end is absolute uncertainty.

2.

a) Kant posits "three unknowables" - a remarkable underestimation - among which he includes freedom. Nietzsche replies by asking: "Not free from what, but free for what?" And elsewhere we can read:

"Freedom is merely a release from bondage, which allows us to choose our own form of

slavery; and it may very well be freedom that we choose."

Precisely this is the paradox of Borges' circular library.

3.

a) The only significant difference between Plato and Schopenhauer is that they are separated by two thousand years of History. And yet, quite clearly, from even a cursory glance at their works, it's Schopenhauer who predates Plato.

b) Recently a friend asked me who I considered to be the greatest contemporary playwright. The question was, of course, fatuous, and deserved a glib reply. For his understanding of human behaviour (I replied, like an emcee at an award ceremony), for the darkness against which he so triumphantly struggles, for the passions that motivate him without ever for a moment coming to rule him, for the Unity to which he aspires and which he occasionally achieves, for the moral forces that drive him, there could be but one choice. He encapsulates both the ugly truths and the extraordinary progress of this terrible century in which good and evil have been pushed to their very limits; he contains all of our hopes and disappointments, all of our dreams and disenchantments; he depicts without flinching the acts of genocidal devastation and the god-like creation; he confronts head-on our failures and our achievements. Only one playwright can claim this laurel: Minamoto no Yorimasa, 12th century Japanese poet of the Noh.

c) The only significant difference between Camus and Shakespeare is that they are separated by three hundred years of History. Shakespeare belonged to a world dominated by religion and monarchy, Camus to a world plunged in doubt and anarchy. The concept of the Absurd not only derives from the latter but is unimaginable as deriving from the former; yet what finer examples of Absurd theatre can we find than "Hamlet", or "Macbeth", than "Timon Of Athens" or "King Lear"?

d) If one is a non-believer, then God is no more than a myth; and men, if not actually free, are at least autonomous. If one is a believer, then God is the great creative imagination, and men - mere figments of that imagination - are but artifices: myths in the mind of God, metaphors for His private light and darkness, inhabitors of his hastily scribbled poem of Earth ("Lord," one of my characters elsewhere prays, "Lord who made the world in less than seven days, why did You not take more time, more care?")

e) Whether one believes in the Big Bang theory of Creation, or in the God in six days theory, is ultimately a matter of faith, and faith is independent of truth or reason. Faith is the kiln in which our necessary illusions are substantiated. Rebbe Wolfe of Zhitomir has written:

"I fail to understand these so-called enlightened people who demand answers, endless answers, in matters of faith. For the believer there is no question; for the non-believer there is no answer."

f) The fact that a man does not believe in God doesn't affect the existence of God in the slightest, but only that of the man. The same is true of ghosts, and quasars, of little green men and quotable writers; of psychoanalysts and essayists as well. The pinnacle of human intelligence is not absolute knowledge, but absolute uncertainty.

g) In the beginning was the myth. And in the end also.

Wolverhampton 1978/Israel 1981/Somerset 1999/Baltimore 2013

ADDENDA

Over the years since I last decided to bring this collection to an end, a number of stories have been delivered to me, several "sender unnamed", but clearly from the infinite storehouses of the extra-terrestrial Muse, others from a named source. Sent to me without requesting payment, how could I refuse so kind and so benevolent an offering? Yet what to do with them, since my book was closed (I would write "finished", but in truth no book is ever finished, but only, as Auden once observed, abandoned), and the symmetry of my preface too neat and too precise to wish to modify it?

I present these few tales, therefore, as addenda to what is already an appendix, conscious that they, once again, repeat some of the themes already explored in previous tales, hopeful that they will nonetheless add at least something to your enjoyment of this occasion upon which you read them.

David Prashker
March 2057

THE PREQUEL

Jean Rhys' novel "The Wild Sargasso Sea" offers a prequel to Jane Eyre's "Wuthering Heights", imagining what might have taken place that led Rochester to be the man he was. John Fowles' novel "The French Lieutenant's Woman", itself "inspired" by the 1823 novel "Ourika", by Claire de Duras (itself a novel published amid much fear that it would be accused of plagiarism), offers three alternate endings, and invites the reader to choose the one that he or she prefers. Thomas Bowdler's versions of the plays of Shakespeare offer happier endings than the originals. I am interested here in the life-work of Chaim Loveh, the author and political commentator, who died last week, aged 89.

During his life Loveh published seven novels; though it may be argued that he only produced one novel, for each bore the same title – "Daniel Deronda" – though each told a very different story. The first repeats, somewhat more briefly and in a more contemporary English, the exact same story of pre-Herzl Zionism that George Eliot told in her original novel of this name. Each of the others follows the lives of the same characters, but each modifies one key incident in the story, and then forms its own judgement of what might have happened next. In one version Daniel does not notice the drowning Mirah, let alone save her; but he does read about her death in the newspaper, at the same time that Sir Hugo Mallinger informs him of his Jewish ancestry, and wandering about Holborn in search of Jewish books in order to learn more, encounters Ezra, makes the connection, and finishes the novel travelling to Palestine. In another version, the constant demands of Gwendolen Grandcourt inspire such pity in him that he abandons his idea of wedding Mirah, and weds Gwendolen instead; the two of them are initially despised in London circles, but his looks and charm, her looks and restored wit, soon make them the centre of London society; the novel ends with Deronda formally converting to Christianity, much to the satisfaction of Mrs Davilow. In a third version guilt finally drives Gwendolen to confessing to the police that Grandcourt's death was no accident; she had deliberately turned the tiller to ensure it struck him on the head; three times she pushed him under with the oar; only when she saw another boat approaching did she dive into the water in order to appear innocent. Deronda, now in Palestine with Mirah, hears from Sir Hugo that she has been sentenced to life in prison, but committed to an insane asylum in lieu of prison, and rushes back to England to be with her. He devotes the remainder of his life to her, while Mirah joins a religious community in Jerusalem. In a fourth version Deronda returns with Mirah; their ship strikes rock near Malta and their tale ends where it began, with Deronda dragging Mirah's body through the water – only this time unsuccessfully. Deronda too loses his sanity, and at Sir Hugo's insistence his mother, the Contessa Maria Alcharisi finally accepts that she has a son, and takes him to Frankfurt to look after him. In a fifth version Grandcourt turns out to have faked his own death, with the full collaboration of the boatmen who dragged his body back to dry land; first in Genoa, then in England, he secretly keeps watch on Gwendolen, convinced she is having an affair with Deronda; and when he sees Deronda out walking with a woman, he assumes it's her, and strikes both down from behind: in fact the woman was Mirah. Grandcourt is arrested and hanged for murder; Sir Hugo files a law-suit against the will, on the grounds that it was written by an insane man; the case wins and Gwendolen inherits the entire estate. She marries Rex and settles down at Offendene.

What each of these versions have in common (and there are, in Loveh's notebooks, some seventeen other alternate versions drafted in some measure, and a further thirty-nine in note form) isn't simply that they rework the story of Daniel Deronda for the purposes of wondering what might have happened; what they share is Loveh's conviction that in all the world there is only one tale, the tale of the human condition; that all renderings of that tale are simply anagrams; that each anagram is simply a set of choices made by this author or that, to suit their personal perspective and agenda, variant in time and place and language, but otherwise the same story.

It seems to me that, in Loveh's work, may lie a cure for writers' work-block, and nutrition for the insatiable appetite of the publishing industry. If all novels are simply anagrams of the same novel, what need to seek originality, when there are so many great books to which any writer can apply Loveh's methodology, either as prequel, sequel or alternative, and for which all the difficult ground-work of plot and character creation has been done for you. Simply take any classic novel, and apply the Loveh method – an infinitude of times. And for the publisher, how much easier to sell a book already known to the reading public, whose nostalgia for their first experience of reading it will readily induce them to return, and find out what alternatives this writer or that one has invented? A thousand versions of Anna Karenina or Great Expectations, of Women In Love or Madame Bovary. I'm particularly keen to read the version of The Forsyte Saga in which Soames does not rape Irene, and would dearly love to know how long Romeo would have remained faithful to Juliet had they lived on and settled down in suburban bliss in Padua.

A WORKABLE UTOPIA

This next came to me by email from ThomasMore@Erasmus.com, an address about which I had considerable doubt until I checked it, and was able to verify its authenticity. It promised a short piece "in what I hope I have imitated fastidiously as your style", and urged it, as the closing line makes apparent, as an addition to my suggestions for interactive literature. I am happy to follow through with this, and once again invite my readers to send their pieces to me care of theargamanpress@yahoo.co.uk, with one qualification, which is that mere anagrams of the failed Utopias of the past will receive the order of the delete button without reply. I include in this category all forms of religion, the absurd theories of Karl Marx and Adam Smith, as well as the literary dogmatisms of John Galt, Emmanuel Goldstein, Henry Ford, or any other Benefactor behind the Green Wall. Below is the piece by Mr More.

It is a feature of the naiveté and disconsolation of all of us that, at some unhappy moment of our lives, we have sought to compensate by conducting in our minds the fantasy of creating a perfect world, understudying the role of God - I note, in passing, that in so doing it's his attribute "omnipotent" and not his characteristic "all-merciful" that we tend to favour - dreaming something that's both perfect, and perfectly in our own image and likeness. As a parlour game, as an analogical structure for serious thought about the "real world", it's an entertaining, even perhaps a cathartic exercise. To write it down, as Condorcet and Rousseau, Washington and Plato have done, is self-indulgent and fatuous, but nothing worse. Mercifully there are few who, like Hitler and Stalin, have sought to apply the working model rather than merely draw the blueprint.

Every utopia is, by definition, untenable, for the very same reason that, if the conditions were right for the coming of the Messiah, then he would of necessity already be here. The dream envisages a perfect circle - but draw a perfect circle and you'll find you have created nought. Utopias which imagine flawlessly benign human beings, all equally dedicated to the establishment of a universe based on total and equal justice, are intrinsically flawed, because they exclude from themselves all normal mortals (there being none who are not flawed), and more particularly any and all of those who do not share the principles of the founder. All Utopias are therefore either desert islands founded on communities of one, or else - and by a curious paradox of logic, liberal Utopias in particular - inherently fascist.

It remains then to create a workable Utopia...

THE MARTYR

I am grateful to the anonymous correspondent – though I have no evidence to support this statement, I believe it is a she, and young – for delivering a series of suggestions for further tales by letter, an old-fashioned means of communication which, as she rightly points out, is appropriate, as the telling of stories in words on a page is itself now an old-fashioned form. But mercifully not yet obsolete.

Amongst the suggestions, all of which relate to tales already in this book (I am particularly intrigued by her hypothesis that the dead man in Simcha Hurlitz's dream may be the second-in-command Colonel Rodrigo; her comment, that the Emperor of the 1001 clocks might have done better to buy a ticket from The Lottery, lacks empathy for the social structures in imperial society), are included two rather maudlin and melancholy pieces, whose tone makes me reluctant to repeat them here, except that their coincidence with the previous tale, "A Workable Utopia", renders it irresistible. Both come in the form of notes, an understandable decision as stories in the form of notes are themselves a leitmotif of this volume, but especially because the development of either tale would likely induce suicidal tendencies in the author. Both carry the same title.

THE MARTYR

Story of the passionate disbeliever who is taken prisoner by the anti-clerical authorities, on charges that have nothing to do with God or atheism. Under torture, because he requires some ideal to struggle for in order to retain his sanity and his physical strength, but mostly as a means of preventing himself from confessing the names and hiding-places of his friends, he pretends a total faith in that God whom the regime is committed to overthrow. So persuasive are his arguments in favour of these views he does not hold, so willing does he show himself to be to die for this God in whom he disbelieves so fervently, his torturers change sides, convince their leaders likewise to transfer allegiance from the anti-clerical to the pro-clerical party, and release him. For the remainder of his life he is obliged to serve as spokesman for the national faith, and dies, aged 98, of natural causes.

THE MARTYR

Two people inhabit a derelict island. Around them are the signs of an established civilisation, but all is in ruins now. As we watch them try to make a life, finding food, arguing constantly, the story slowly emerges, of an attempt to build a moral universe.

They remind us of:

* the announcement of the dawn of the messianic age, which we, your government, will bring into being. It is full of moral and ethical values, and a determination to rid the planet of all forms of evil;

* the return of the death penalty, automatic for murderers, traitors, and anyone who carried weaponry for criminal purposes, even if they didn't use it;

* the clamour of the people against the country's participation in wars elsewhere: we make the guns, and sell them; we are profiting from the deaths of other people; it has to stop. So the making of guns, and the selling of guns, was outlawed, as were all other weapons, with the exception of those needed by the army to defend the land against any who thought it was becoming weak and therefore vulnerable, and the means of carrying out death sentences;

* the clamour of the people against profiteers and speculators, wife-beaters and child-abusers, prostitutes and pimps, adulterers and tax-evaders, corrupt politicians and bankers, bullying lawyers and scientists willing to prove anything their research funder requires…

And so it goes on, death sentence after death sentence, until there are just the two of them left, one the former president of the republic, who announced the messianic age and introduced the death penalty, the other the former leader of the opposition…

Who now takes out the last gun left, declares the former President a brutal murderer, shoots him, and then kills himself.

THE LIBRARY AT BABEL

In my story "A Don Juan of the Imagination", these words are recorded:

"The key," he told me, "isn't to read, but to re-read. No book, no work of art, no suite of music, is ever the same twice. The fact that we've encountered it before changes our apprehension of it on the next occasion. And besides, encountering it makes us different, alters our inner state, and so it's never the same person who is making the encounter."

It therefore intrigued me to receive the following story from another correspondent:

THE LIBRARY AT BABEL

We did not intend to build this library. Our aim was greater than that. Our aim was to construct the Tower of Babel. But God intervened. He confused our language, so we could not communicate the plans for the Tower. A meeting was convened, to discuss what should be done, but none of us could understand the proposals, and so, by the tacit agreement of silence, the Tower was abandoned.

Unaware that I was not alone in this endeavour, I set out to create a perfect language (this is not it), one with which God could not interfere, one which would restore our powers of communication and thus enable us to resume the project. It has taken many years, but already there are several of us who have understood the basic problems. Between us we have gathered copies of all the books that exist, and have written countless more ourselves. That is why we built this library, which, as you can see, is so vast that it will soon reach the very gates of Heaven.

ABOUT THE AUTHOR

David Prashker was born in London in 1955 and has lived in France, Israel, Canada and the United States, where he is currently based.

He is the author of thirty books, including contemporary and historical novels, short stories, poetry, songs, plays and scholarly works. You can follow his blog at apps.theargamanpress.com/Blog/ or find him at his website Davidprashker.com. For more information about his books, go to
theargamanpress.com.